The Misaaventures
of Sister Mary Olga Fortitude

DAVIS AUJOURD'HUI

Outskirts Press, Inc.
Denver, Colorado

Outskirts Press, Inc.
http://www.outskirtspress.com

ISBN: 978-1-4327-3047-5

Dedicated to all adult children
who deserve the chance to not take life so seriously
as well as to the memory of Janice M. Reilly
who will always be Sister Mary Olga to me

Foreword

T.L.I.A.M.G., my dears! This is Sister Mary Olga Fortitude coming to you. Now! I should let you know what T-LIAM-G stands for. It is an acronym that means The Lord Is A Mighty God! Well, we all should know that by now, but some of us have seemed to have conveniently forgotten that. Well, my dears, that is why I'm going to tell you my story since I am a good and holy teacher. I'm here to remind you that all of us have been called to serve in this life. Of course, some of you seem to expect to be served by others. Well, it's time to wake up and smell the whiskey...er, I mean the coffee!

Now! I want each of you to sit back and take a deep breath. That's right, my dears! Fill your lungs up with the very life breath of God. That should be a humbling experience since you wouldn't have any breath unless God gave it to you. Now, don't feel too guilty if you've forgotten that; unless, of course, you feel that you need to!

I must make a confession to you. I have a particular view that it's most holy to use the lungs in a variety of ways. I like to use my breath to direct my prayers and I feel it's particularly holy to offer up smoke signals to the Lord. Of course, our current Reverend Mother doesn't approve of that and I don't expect your mothers would approve either. Let's just say that I'm set in my ways and I don't always see eye to eye with authority figures. It's just that I have a passion for my Marlboros; but, you didn't hear that from me!

I guess that I should tell you a little bit about myself before I get up on my soapbox. After all, I have a story of grace to share with you as we all do. Perhaps I can shed a little love light by telling you about some of my adventures which will hopefully inspire you to practice holiness in your own particular fashions. After all, each of us is unique and we all have something special to offer!

As real as this story and these characters may seem to you, I must confess that this is a work of fiction. Names, characters, places, and incidents are the product of this author's imagination or are used fictitiously; and, any resemblance to actual persons, living or dead, events, or locales is entirely coincidental. Yet, I must add that, in God's universe, everything is perfectly ordered, there are no coincidences, and everything happens for a reason.

Chapter 1

I live at the Have A Heart Convent which is located in a little town called Bucksnort. Perhaps it's a town much like your own, but that doesn't really matter. It's a humble and hallowed place in the upper part of Wisconsin. Here in our local parish, I teach young children to live by the Golden Rule. The only problem which I have discovered is that most adults behave more like children than children do. If you're one of these unfortunate souls, then this book is especially for you!

I was born sixty-five years ago on February twenty-ninth. That would have been 1940. Since that year was a leap year, I've only had sixteen birthdays and one unbirthday since then. That works to my advantage now since I can tell the children I'm sweet sixteen; but, let me tell you, I got into a real snit about that as a child!

Since February twenty-ninth rolls around just once every four years, I only got to celebrate my birthday once in a blue moon as a child. It's not that my parents were particularly mean, but they went according to the book and the calendar. For them to have broken the rules would have been as if it was a sin! They'd rub it in even further when they'd say, "It's more blessed to give than it is to receive."

I was four years old before I got to celebrate my first

birthday. Yet every year, I'd be invited to other friends' birthday parties. There, I would have to watch them be showered with the very presents I would have liked to have received. Then, I'd have to wait out those four interminable years before I got my own party. Let's just say that my parents and those other nasty children didn't make up for lost time when it came to giving presents to me!

What only made matters worse was that my so-called friends would make such a big deal about each of their own presents. There was a family of girls, the Mayhem sisters, who had a birthday each month of spring. Mildred was the oldest and she had her birthday in March. Martha Mayhem was my age. Her birthday would come each April. Myrtle Mayhem was the baby of the family and she was born on Memorial Day.

The Mayhem girls also had an older brother named Mark. He would always say my middle name of "Olga" in such a mocking way that I grew to detest it. He would taunt me when he'd sarcastically say, "Poor little Mary OLGA only gets a birthday once every four years!"

The worst offender was a vile little girl named Priscilla Bunhead. Prissy would always run out of her house whenever she saw me coming. Every time, she'd rub salt into my wounds by saying, "I've got a new dolly!" or "Look at my new dress!"

Well, I got even with her one day. I grabbed that new dolly out of her hands and I pulled all of the hair out of its little china head. In the process, I managed to behead that pretty little doll! That served her right!

My parents didn't think so. I got coal in my stocking that Christmas since they decided to teach me a lesson. That really made me fume! At least I was able to get some satisfaction when I used it to get even with Mark Mayhem. The next time he mocked my name, I threw that big lump of coal at him and hit him in his handsome head. It wasn't so handsome afterwards. He ended up with a lump on his head that was almost as big as the lump that hit him!

When my friends turned twenty-one, they were able to legally drink; but, my parents insisted that I couldn't since they claimed it wasn't appropriate for a five-year-old to do so! Well, I didn't let that stop me! The bars and liquor stores didn't apply the same stupid rules to the calendar; so, I just kept a secret stash in a cubbyhole in my closet. I also resolved that I was going to move out of my parents' home before my next un-birthday!

I had always been a good girl, but I wasn't going to put up with any more rubbish! Since I held a special place in my heart for Jesus, I decided I was going to become a nun. The only problem was that I was a Baptist. That's another story!

I started attending the local Catholic church and I talked with the priest about my desire to convert. Of course, I had to make up for lost time by making a very long confession. At least my penance was no big deal. He told me I should become a nun. Well, that was easy. I'd already decided I wanted to do that! My parents threw a fit, but I didn't care. I'd already written a letter to the Reverend Mother of the Have A Heart convent and she offered me refuge.

So, I headed out into the world by leaving the world behind and I became a novice at the convent which has served as my humble home ever since. I took the name of Sister Mary Olga Fortitude and I soon became a favorite of The Reverend Mother. Even though she tried hard to be impartial, I especially liked the way she addressed me in private. She called me "Moffy." I finally felt as if I was truly loved.

Chapter 2

Wouldn't you know it, some of the other novices were even nastier than the children who had been so stingy with their presents to me as a child. There was one novice in particular to whom I took a special dislike. God forgive me, but I judged her for her past. Her name was Sister Carmen Magdalena Burana and she had been a common streetwalker before she took holy solace at the convent. I must confess that I devised a secret name for her. That name was "N.B.A.W." In my mind that translated to Nothing But A Whore.

I prayed to God to rid me of my judgmental thoughts, but that soon became one of my many crosses to bear. Sister Carmen was a good actress. She perfected the role of perfect piety in public, but her true colors blazed in private. She was haughty and ambitious. She was also jealous of my relationship with the Reverend Mother. She'd belittle me and mock me in private.

All I could do was to take my ever-increasing judgments to confession with Father Nosebest. I didn't want to admit my weakness to the Reverend Mother. I was afraid that she'd only think less of me. I had one other way to cope with my growing resentments toward Sister Carmen. I'd take every opportunity I could to sneak a smoke and to drink my private stash of Old Granddad.

In the last years before I'd made my escape to the sanctuary of the convent, I'd made quick friends with spirits other than the Holy Spirit. I became especially fond of whiskey. That delicious taste of bourbon would linger on my palate unlike any other liquor. I had also started smoking in secret and I loved to wash down a few puffs of smoke with the sweet warmth of the liquid fire of that very affordable bourbon. God, forgive me, but they were absolutely delicious!

I'd sneak out to the privacy of our privy where I could chain smoke and secretly imbibe while pretending to be in contemplative prayer. Yes, sad but true, my parents were so frugal that we were the only house in the neighborhood without indoor plumbing! At least I'd discovered one way to turn that source of embarrassment to my advantage, making it my secret getaway. The rank odor of the outhouse was a clever disguise for my form of fervent prayer.

My parents were aghast that I was converting to Catholicism, but I hoped that they would consider it to be the lesser of the other evils that could seduce a young girl during the 1950's. At least I wasn't shrieking in delight or writhing on the floor like the Mayhem girls whenever they played their Elvis Presley records. I also wasn't teasing my hair into a rat's nest like Priscilla Bunhead. All of that was the work of the devil as far as my parents were concerned. Of course, becoming a Catholic was only one step short of perdition to them.

You may wonder how I managed to indulge in my secret "vices" once I joined the convent. Well, it won't hurt me now to tell you how I went about that. I volunteered to do the weekly shopping with our deliveryman who just happened to be a former schoolmate of mine. He was also someone over whom I could hold something in exchange for his confidence.

When I should have been sweet sixteen, Diddles Dinkledorf mocked me endlessly because I was the only girl of that age who had never been kissed. Well, as my fortune would have it, I caught him in a compromising position a few years later. On one of my secret spiritual getaways to the privy, I discovered Diddles diddling Mark Mayhem in our outhouse. This was long before the days of gay liberation.

My discovery gave me an advantage when I needed my own cover of secrecy; I'll get to that in awhile. Mind you, it's not that there's anything wrong with that kind of behavior. It's just that people saw these kinds of affairs differently in the 1950's. Still, who was I to judge? I must confess that I also got a secret satisfaction over having caught that nasty Mark Mayhem with his pants down. Lord, forgive me!

Whenever shopping day would arrive, I would be in high spirits and filled with anticipation. God knows, I needed something to quell my ever-increasing resentments toward Sister Carmen. I'd meet Diddles at the convent gate with shopping list in hand. I'd also slip him my own secret order for a carton of Marlboros and a quart of Old Granddad. Off we'd go in the convent's Buick station wagon. It would only be a short two hours later when we arrived back with the groceries which I'd quickly put away so that I could sneak off to indulge myself. God forgive me!

You may wonder how I managed to go undetected. I must admit I was pretty clever. God forgive me for my vanity. When I first arrived at the convent, I noticed a small, ramshackle structure in the adjacent overgrown field that was all too familiar. Even though the convent had all the modern conveniences, there was a vestige of its primitive past in that field. It was a beautifully-appointed six-seater privy, complete with an adjacent prayer room.

Old habits die hard and God knows my habits were all too well-established at this point in my young life. I'd made it known to the Reverend Mother that I had a particular passion for offering up private prayers in the most humble of circumstances. I told her that I'd noticed the old privy and that I'd taken the liberty of checking it out as a reminder of my humble past.

I confessed my past sin of resenting my parents for making me perform "my necessaries" in a privy. I suggested that the old convent privy's prayer room would be the perfect place for me to practice penance by offering up my humble prayers while there. The dear Reverend Mother agreed that would be a perfect solution in order to absolve myself.

I now had my secret hideaway in which none of the other nuns or novices would be caught dead. Since four seemed to be my number, the fourth seat in the privy became my new cubbyhole for my secret stash. After evening vespers, I would venture out in the dark to my private prayer room. There, I would offer up fervent prayers with an endless chain of smoke from my Marlboros. There, I would also quench my parched throat with the liquid nectar of my bourbon. God forgive me for my deception.

As time went by, I earned extra favor from the Reverend Mother by making more frequent vigils to that humble haven. In the light of the early morning dawn, the Reverend Mother would smile at me from her convent window as I made my pilgrimage to the privy potties. Lord, did I ever feel guilty!

Not to worry, I soon assuaged my guilt in fervent prayer which I washed down with my ever increasing stash of spirits. Of course, if I got carried away during my evening ritual, I'd have quite a brutal reminder in the form of a major hangover the next morning. Fortunately, I could deal with that by embracing the old remedy of the hair of the dog during my morning prayer vigils – a couple of good snorts of Old Granddad.

As the time drew near for me to take my final vows, I found myself ever more drawn to the Holy Spirit as well as to my own stash of spirits. I wondered if there wouldn't be a way to indulge myself on a more regular basis without making unnecessary trips to the necessary room. I finally had a brainstorm.

Diddles Dinkledorf had his own past to overcome and had sought to find other ways to be of service to the Lord in which he could absolve his own guilt. Even though he had since married and had started populating the town with new Dinkledorf Catholics, he still remained a "good buddy" with Mark Mayhem.

Diddles had become an apprentice at the religious artifacts craft shop, located on the convent grounds. One of the many artifacts he had learned to create were the beautiful large crucifixes which were presented to new nuns. Diddles had remained in my debt in exchange for my confidence concerning his "good buddy" This served as an inspiration to me for my brainstorm.

I asked Diddles if it would be possible for him to create a custom crucifix for me. I advised him that it had to be an otherwise exact replica of the crucifixes created for the nuns. What I had in mind was a particularly hollow version of our suffering Lord. I asked him to create mine with a flip-top cross so that I could fill my crucifix with a little something to quench my ever-increasing thirst. Diddles proved to be a true craftsman and he created an exact replica of those crucifixes, but mine was retrofitted with a handy flip-top.

I was beaming with fervent joy on the day I finally received it. A short while later, I anointed my cross with its first baptism of my spirits. Each day thereafter, I would reverently fill that crucifix to the brim of its flip-top. It would serve as a tangible example that my fortitude could always come from the cross of Jesus.

I quickly developed the habit of kissing my cross. What the other nuns did not know, at the time, was that I had finessed the technique of flicking the top of the cross with my teeth and having myself a quick snort along with my reverent kiss. I was a bride of Christ and captive to the spirits within his cross. This would become my lifelong cross to bear.

Chapter 3

*T*he days passed slowly while I waited out the hours between my morning and evening vigils. Even so, that elusive quality of time made the years pass swiftly. Somehow I managed to remain in the good graces of the Reverend Mother. That dear old soul never guessed my well-kept secret vices. I wasn't so lucky when it came to the worldly guile of Sister Carmen. It hadn't taken her very long to figure out that my prayer sessions involved spirits other than the Holy Spirit. Still, she remained ignorant about the extra blessing contained in my crucifix.

I must say, God is good! As my good fortune would have it, I soon received the blessing of something to hold over Sister Carmen as well. Old habits die hard. That "good" sister had another lingering habit which was far from holy in her case. Now! I'm not a gossip or a snitch, but I am human, after all, and I had to protect my own secret.

On one beautiful moonlit night, I decided to throw caution to the wind and I took my bottle of Old Granddad for a stroll. It was a balmy night and I was filled with more than just the Holy Spirit. The stars were shining like tiny diamonds in the night sky and a full moon illuminated the surrounding countryside. As I ventured out into the field behind the privy, I discovered a freshly worn path; so, I took off on an adventure as I sent up smoke signals to God from my trusty Marlboros.

Oh, I was feeling such rushes of ecstasy! I was enthralled with the natural beauty of the countryside as I weaved and wobbled along the path that led toward the nearby woods. Eventually, the path meandered alongside a wide babbling brook that gurgled with pure delight. I wanted to walk on top of the large rocks within that flowing stream bed, but I didn't trust my balance since Old Granddad was having his way with me. It wouldn't be long before I discovered someone having his way with Sister Carmen.

Off in the distance I noticed an old stone building with an ancient water wheel. I figured this must have been the old mill for the convent. The path I was following indeed appeared to be freshly downtrodden and I became quite curious when I noticed the soft flickering light of a candle which danced upon the thick and wavy ancient glass of the window of the mill.

As I drew nearer, I became aware of what sounded like some most unusual wild animal noises. My pulse quickened and I must confess I lost faith for a minute. I became afraid. Nevertheless, my curiosity got the best of me. I took a bracing slug from Old Granddad and I tiptoed toward the mill from which those sounds seemed to be coming.

I suddenly became aware that those sounds were not from animals at all. I quickly discovered that something other than grain was grinding at the mill! I tiptoed alongside the cool stone structure and I surreptitiously peered in through the dusty windowpane.

The flickering light of the candle illuminated my virginal eyes. There, in the throes of her own ecstasy, was Sister Carmen with a big strapping man, colored in shades reminiscent of the cafe au laits we enjoyed at breakfast. I recognized him immediately. It was none other than Jules Jesslike Pappas. He was the older, biracial half-brother of our local celebrity radio chef, Amanda Ann Adult. The Lord is a mighty God; T-LIAM-G! Now I had one on that N.B.A.W., Sister Carmen! Lord, forgive me for my judgment!

I must confess that I felt a twinge of envy over Sister Carmen's obvious joy, but I took my vows seriously and I would remain true to my vow of chastity. Apparently, some of us only maintain our vows when it's convenient! Sister Carmen's former profession seemed to have served her well. Diddles Dinkledorf and Mark Mayhem couldn't hold a candle to the likes of this copulating couple. Lord have mercy!

I smiled a secret smile as I tiptoed and tottered away from that building. That smile never left my face as I made my return moonlit trip to the convent. I decided I would have to pay a visit on Sister Carmen at her cell after light's out. Not that I approve of blackmail, but I wasn't going to take a chance that she might ruin my relationships with Old Granddad or the Reverend Mother by disclosing my own secrets.

The following years passed swiftly and I settled into the tranquility of my life at the convent. Yet, while God is good, the Lord giveth and the Lord taketh away. On another beautiful moonlit night, God took our blessed Reverend Mother from us. She passed on to her reward peacefully, in her sleep. God bless her soul. Life was about to change and not for the better, in my humble opinion!

I had passed my forty-eighth unbirthday and I was now twelve years old, according to my worldly parents. By the time of my actual thirteenth birthday, I would have endured a most unpleasant and humiliating surprise. After all of my years of piety thinking I would make a perfect Reverend Mother, I received a lesson in humility. Sister Carmen was promoted, leaving me in the ranks of humiliation. Thirteen indeed became an unlucky number for me; not that I'm superstitious! Oh, my God! The Lord does work in mysterious ways!

Chapter 4

T-LIAM-G, my dears! This is Sister Mary Olga Fortitude coming you. Now! I'm feeling very humble indeed. Here I am on my knees in my convent cell. This is my penance from the "Reverend" Mother Carmen Burana. When I arrived at morning chapel with an obvious hangover, I received a knowing look from the new Reverend Mother. I prayed that I would be able to escape her wrath this day, but the Lord had other plans in store for me. Mother Carmen caught up with me as I was scurrying out of the chapel and she advised me to wait for her in her chambers.

When she arrived, she appeared to be nearly gloating. Sashaying toward her throne, with her crucifix swaying wildly to and fro, she seated herself as if she was a queen. Lord knows, I've met some queens in this life who were more regal than she! I knew what was coming and I braced myself for another dose of her own form of piety.

Mother opened her voluptuous mouth to speak and then she said, "Sister Mary OLGA Fortitude! When are you ever going to learn? Not only are you a disgrace to the convent, but you continue to incessantly demonstrate the most stubborn willfulness before your Lord. If your drunken debauchery wasn't enough, what about the money you waste upon impure spirits that could have been used to help the unfortunate of our parish? Where is your loyalty to those in need? Where is your service to your Lord and Savior? How can I get it through that thick wimple of yours that enough is enough?"

I was squirming in my seat with my disdain for this pompous hypocrite. I thought to myself, "God forgive me for my judgment, but I'm calling a spade a spade. I only wished that I had had hip boots and a shovel to deal with this sanctimonious sister!"

I wasn't about to further humiliate myself by answering. Besides, I knew she only wanted to hear herself speak. Mother Carmen didn't miss a beat in her continuing diatribe. The only thing that made the situation more oppressive was the atmosphere of the newly decorated Mother's chambers. The formerly warm and cheerful room of my blessed departed Reverend Mother had been draped in cascades of ebony even darker than the very habits we wore.

I thought to myself again, "Mirror, mirror on the wall, who is the wickedest witch of them all?" If I only had had the gumption to kiss my crucifix flask and have a quick snort, I could have settled my nerves for an instant. I knew what was coming next.

Once again, Mother opened her churlish lips and said, "Sister, it's time for you to give something back to the Lord. I want you to go to your cell for the remainder of the day. You will fast, you will kneel on the bare floor, and you will meditate upon your transgressions until evening vespers. You may go now!"

I slunk away from her chambers feeling as if I had been soiled. How could this be happening to me? I should have become the Reverend Mother. Well Lord, I guess this is another cross of mine to bear and I will gladly do it for you. Her day of reckoning will be reward enough for me.

I spoke out loud to Jesus, "How will I get through the rest of the day with the tiny flask of spirits contained in your own cross of sorrow? Forgive me, Lord. How can I feel sorry for myself when I consider the throes of agony that you endured?" That put everything into perspective. At least, I had something other than vinegar with which to quench my parched throat.

So, my dears, there it was, God only knows how many hours later and I was still kneeling on my aching bended knees. I was hungry and I was waiting for the chapel bell to signal the end of my penance. I must admit, I was feeling rather holy. There was and always is something to be said for reflection.

Of course, I had no intention of repenting from my secret pleasures. God forgive me. After all, I needed something to steady my nerves when dealing with Mother Carmen. Yet, I did believe I was now in a better position to teach my classes in Advanced Holiness. After all, I had spent more time in solitary contemplation than all of the other sisters combined.

There was one practical dilemma that I had to solve as soon as possible upon Sister Carmen's promotion. Since she knew of my secret hiding place, I had to find somewhere else to store my stash. That was a relatively easy problem to solve. I simply let God lead me to cubicle number four of the convent rest room.

By now, four happened to be my second favorite number. Three had become my new favorite because it represented the Holy Trinity. In keeping with my previous tradition, cubicle number four became my new hiding place. There, in that modern privy, I stashed my bottle of Old Granddad in the toilet tank.

At least Mother Carmen hadn't figured out how I had been getting my liquor supplied. Diddles valued his secret affair with Mark Mayhem more than he valued getting honest with Mother Carmen. It had made it even easier that he didn't like her any more than I did. The reason for that was that Mark had confessed that he'd tricked with Mother Carmen before she had gotten religious.

My biggest challenge had been finding the opportunities in which to send up smoke signals to God. Mother Carmen hadn't approved of that pastime either. As a result, I had been forced to literally chain smoke any opportunity that I got. I'd never know when I'd have a chance for my next fix.

I wonder if the chain smoking has anything to do with the raspy nature of my voice? Well, I don't have to sing any solos. I'm content to sing in the choir of angels!

Chapter 5

*H*ow time does fly! It's now 2005 and I am sixteen birthdays plus one unbirthday old. I am so present to the moment that it makes me feel every one of my sixty-five years on this earth. Consequently, I am at the point where I began my story.

I've been teaching the young children of our parish for over forty years now. I also teach classes in Advanced Holiness to the oldest children, as well as to some of the higher-minded adults of our little community. I can thank the other dear sisters of the convent for helping me to hold onto this class. Mother Carmen had planned to strip that teaching assignment away from me as a punishment, but the rest of the convent rallied behind me. God bless their souls!

I adore the little children, but of course there are always at least a couple of behavioral problems. Wouldn't you know it! My latest challenge is the grandson of Diddles Dinkledorf. I must admit that the little lad has been suitably named, though I'll never understand how the parish priest allowed him to be baptized with his name. On second thought, I bet I have the answer for that one. The new padre has turned out to share my passion for bourbon.

I made that discovery when I took a nostalgic trip to the

privy in the field. I heard a ruckus within and I went inside to investigate. A very tipsy Father Cowberries had tried to relieve himself in the old outhouse and then had lost his balance, falling headfirst into one of the latrines. How he had ever managed to do that I will not know! Anyhow, I became his savior when I hoisted him out of that unhallowed hole and he became mine since I spent a lot of time in confession.

It wasn't long thereafter before the two of us each had our own cubbyholes in the confessional. That ensured that my confessions would become even more fruitful for both of us when refreshed with a few good snorts.

I also received some of my own training in Advanced Holiness during these sessions. After we both had tipped our bottles throughout my long-winded confessions, Father Cowberries would ask me if I would hear his confession. Lord, that priest had a checkered past! It's a good thing that I took the vow of the confessional seriously because he told me stories you would not believe. Well, you didn't hear that from me. Don't tell the Pope that this sister has been serving in the role of a priest!

Now, where was I? Oh yes, I was going to tell you about the little Dinkledorf boy. Would you believe it? His parents named him Fartley! But, like I said, he has been well-named.

That little boy is the most flatulent child I've ever known. The most unsettling thing about him is that he seems to take a particularly perverse pleasure in passing gas. He is constantly letting go whenever I start lecturing on a particularly serious subject. What only makes matters worse is that he always lets out a giggle of delight whenever he interjects his offensive trademark.

Lord knows, I've tried everything to break him of the habit. At first, I sent him to the class bathroom, but that only made matters worse. He'd fluff away while in there.

Now, wait just a minute, Sister! Let's tell it like it is. If you'll pardon the expression, he'd fart away in that vast tiled bathroom with such an exuberance that the echoes would ricochet off the walls with a reverberation that could be palpably felt as I was attempting to write on the quaking blackboard! Nothing that I have since tried has worked. Let's just say that he keeps my habit in an uproar and we'll leave it at that!

I suppose that poor little Fartley is an example of the sins of the fathers being passed down to the sons. After all, his grandfather is a diddler. Talk about karma coming back through that unfortunate child's rear end! Aside from Fartley's flatulent ways, he is also obsessed with bathroom humor. God surely knows what a bad influence that he has had on the other dear children!

Many of these children are the grandchildren of the children with whom I'd grown up. Amazingly, many of them are dear hearts. I actually have had more problems with their parents and grandparents. As for these so-called adults, some of these lost souls actually thought they could buy a ticket into heaven by taking one of my classes in Advanced Holiness. God help them!

Where shall I begin? Well, you've heard me talk about the notorious Mark Mayhem. Perhaps you may remember that he had three sisters. My biggest challenge next to Mother Carmen herself is Mark's sister, Martha Mayhem. Martha is an old maid and she is one of the most cantankerous members of my class. Let me try to paint you a picture for you.

Do you remember the cartoon character, Crabby Appleton? Well, he would have met his match in Martha. Martha doesn't have a kind word to say about anyone and she's always complaining or whining about something. Of course, I've found secret pleasure whenever she would start complaining about Mother Carmen. Lord, forgive me.

Martha thinks that Mother Carmen is a sanctimonious snob. Well, I haven't been about to argue with her. To argue with one wouldn't be very holy, now would it?

The only problem is that Martha always tries to monopolize my classes with her tirades about other people. Actually, I think that she has served as a perfect example of what not to do if one is to be holy; but, I can't very easily point that out to the class. Let's just hope that those students whose light bulbs aren't too dim can make that connection.

Speaking of connections, I've always had to run to the confessional after a class whenever Martha Mayhem has been present. God knows I've had to let go of one judgment after another with Father Cowberries. Not that I have minded in the least. I was getting to be pretty fond of our confessions since the refreshments were always excruciating. That's meant to be a bit of humor since I've learned that one needs to be patient concerning one's shortcomings. The only thing that was excruciating about my refreshments was when my flip-top flask ran dry. Then, again, I'd often have to pay the piper on the day after. Never mind!

Another challenge in my classroom has been that of the closed-minded Priscilla Bunhead. She has long since abandoned her fashion of teasing her hair, but she has paid a price for that vanity. After her teenage years of teasing her hair, it would not lay flat no matter what she did with it. Consequently, the only hair option remaining for her had become to tie her hair down into a tight little bun. I must admit that I found that to be a fitting end for that formerly spoiled child whose dolly got her hair yanked out by yours truly.

I nearly flipped my wimple when Jules Jesslike Pappas walked into my classroom one evening. I struggled to keep that image of him down by the old mill stream out of my brain. He was still a virile-looking specimen of manhood even now that he is in his eighties. I must confess I've entertained fantasies of serving him as Sister Carmen had done during some of my weaker moments.

On those mornings when I was hung over and staring into my cafe au lait, I'd be able to let go of my throbbing head by thinking of him. If Mother Carmen only knew what had been going through my brain during one of her ensuing lectures, perhaps even she would blush! God only knows the torments that I went through as thoughts of Jules lingered and provided me with comforting diversion while serving out another sentence of penitence on my sore and bended knees. Lord forgive me for my impure thoughts.

Chapter 6

*N*ot that I want to gossip, but I thought it might be
illuminating to you judgment-casters to hear the
story of how Jules came to be. It's a tale stranger than a
side show at a carnival. Now! Where should I begin?

I'm quite sure that I mentioned Jules has a younger
sister named Amanda Ann Adult who is our local radio
chef. Well, I should also let you know that he has a twin
sister. She's really rather famous. She was once a popular
movie star, but I'd prefer not to name names. Let's just say
that this sister served as an inspiration to Amanda Ann who
sought the same kind of fame for herself. Unfortunately for
Amanda Ann, she had always fallen a few steps short.

This only served to make Amanda Ann jealous. Could
she have missed my lesson on the seven deadly sins?
Amanda Ann got a chip on her shoulder that was bigger
than a dowager's hump. The stew was brewing and
Amanda Ann, true to her professional calling, was the chef.
It's just that Amanda Ann's stew was never complete until
she "got stewed" herself. Let's tell it like it is, Amanda Ann
is a drunk! But, who am I to judge? I guess you could just
say, it takes one to know one!

Anyhow, as rumor has it, Jules and his twin sister both
had different fathers. Their mother, May I. Doomutch, was

a simple woman who paid no attention to social conventions and was rather loose in her ways. I've always wondered if she might not be the mother of another illegitimate child. Well, if I'm going to protect that adult child's identity, let's just say that she made a living from her loose ways and she has since tried to buy a ticket into heaven by becoming a nun! Enough said!

Now, where was I? Ah yes, I was talking about the twins' less than holy conception. Their wayward mother, forgive me for my judgment, was the product of an incestuous relationship. Her parents shall remain nameless. The consequence of that relationship was that the poor child was about as bright as Thomas Edison's first light bulb. Well, here we go again! It's another lesson about the sins of the fathers being passed down to the sons; or rather, to the poor daughter in this case.

Good Lord, here I am talking about the twins' grandparents! I'll just kiss my crucifix and see if the Lord will help me obtain some mental clarity. Ah yes, that's much better! T-LIAM-G! Now! Their mother, May I. Doomutch, has lived up to her name. As a young child, she would always be asking, "May I do this?" or "May I do that?" By the time she had become an adult, she always answered that question for herself with a resounding, "Yes!" Well, she has more than lived up to her last name of Doo-mutch!

May I. was certainly doing much on the night of the twins' conception. She was a free spirit and she had sexual relations with two men that night. One of the men was white and the other man was black. As fate would have it, and surely the Lord didn't mind, both of those men became fathers nine months later. The girl child came out vanilla and Jules came out chocolate.

Simple-minded May gave the children names that reminded her of their fathers. God bless her soul. Call it stereotypical if you will, but May I. let out a shout of joy when she was presented with that little boy who did NOT have a little member.

When the nurse held up that little baby for the first time for his mother to see, she asked May, "What will you name him?"

May was still marveling over the little baby's big jewels and she exclaimed, "Jewels jus' like Pappa's!"

Well now! That was the name that went on the baby's birth certificate, though it read, "Jules Jesslike Pappas." That's just what May had had in mind. She was proud of her boy and she wanted him to be proud of every part of himself. He deserved a strong name!

Well, my dears, we all are fond and proud of May I's less than famous children. They have both proved to be upstanding members of our community; no pun intended in Jules' case! All of the good housewives, not to mention some of our openly gay men, have Amanda Ann to thank for inspiring them to be better cooks.

That certainly has not turned out to be the case for Diddles Dinkledorf and Mark Mayhem. The only cooking they seem to know how to do continues to be reenacted in the abandoned privy of my childhood home. You didn't hear that from me! Given their fake macho images, one could say they've been doing their cooking in the closet; and, it's not a water closet, I can assure you! Well, if I'm going to keep to my lessons in Advanced Holiness, I guess I should say, "To each their own."

I must say that I've enjoyed helping Amanda Ann in the convent kitchen when she comes to lend her talents for our annual Christmas pageant. She always prepares such a lovely table of tantalizing food. It's just that she's often under the table by the time the food is served.

Her holiday egg nog is always so temptingly delicious that I must confess I tend to overindulge myself. Now, I'm not going to say that she spikes the egg nog she serves to the children, but she always makes a generous private stash for the two of us. Then, Father Cowberries always manages to show up like clockwork as the last of the bourbon, rum, and brandy is poured into the brew.

It's unfortunate for the sisters of the Have A Heart convent that Amanda Ann never became a nun. She's another unfortunate spinster in our community which only serves to give her another reason to drink.

When Amanda Ann's not around, we have a former cowboy who dishes up the grub at the convent. Let me assure you, I'm being kind when I use that term! Randy Cowboy's idea of a gourmet meal is western eggs and hash browns. It's no wonder that half the sisters have cholesterol counts going through the roof!

Randy Cowboy is another story and I'll save that one for another day. It's nearly time for evening vespers and I'm most anxious to spend some time in the confessional with Father Cowberries afterwards. God knows I'm a sinner; and, aside from a baptism, there's nothing more cleansing than a nice stiff drink...er, confession with Father! T-LIAM-G!

Chapter 7

I guess it would be appropriate to tell you the story of Randy Cowboy and Father Cowberries. First of all, I should tell you that they're cousins. Now! You may wonder about their similar, yet different, last names. Well! The truth is that they are both Cowberries, but Randy is the perennial cowboy who never outgrew his love for playing cowboys and Indians. In fact, he still loves to play with other adult boys who've never outgrown that passion. Consequently, he has taken liberties with his given name in order to help him act out his own fantasies.

Now! Let me just say that I have nothing personal against people who live in a fantasy world. It's just that Randy's cowboy fantasies are more along the lines of the Village People. Unlike Diddles Dinkledorf and Mark Mayhem, Randy burst out of his closet as a young teen. God bless his soul! Randy had proved to be very authentic in that regard.

Of course, we need to have compassion for the likes of those unfortunate individuals who don't have the courage to be true to themselves. I'm referring to those closet cases, Diddles and Mark. All we can do is to pray for them.

I hope you realize that I'm going out on a limb with my philosophies about gay people. I don't even mind if you tell the Pope! I'd like to know what's in his closet that causes him to cast judgments against others of God's children. The same goes for anyone who expresses disdain or fear of something about which they know nothing; or, that they're afraid to face within themselves. Surely, that's another lesson in Advanced Holiness!

I'm beating around the bushes again. Pardon me while I just have myself a little liquid refreshment in order to clear my thoughts. Ah! That's much better! Thank you, Jesus! Let's just say that Randy Cowboy has had some "bush issues" too. What's more, he's always lived up to his first name. Randy's what you might call a sex maniac and he's proud of it. Well, who am I to judge? As much as I've been tempted, I've always lived up to my vow of chastity.

When Randy's not slinging up the hash, he's off to the big city wearing only a pair of chaps. You'd think the poor boy's ample buns would get chapped on a cold winter's evening! Anyway, that's our little secret. We wouldn't want Mother Carmen to get wise to his secret pleasures. Then again, how could she be in any position to cast a judgment, given her own past?

When Randy's at work, he always does his job well; so, who should care what he does in his personal life as long as he doesn't hurt anyone else? I must confess that I have other reasons to like Randy. He's a generous soul and he always brings me back a bottle of Jack Daniels whenever he goes to the big city. I wouldn't even mind if he made extra trips there on weeknights!

Now! Randy's actually a first cousin once-removed from Father Cowberries. Randy's father, God rest his soul, was their father's (not the one which art in Heaven) younger first cousin. The two of them were both altar boys at the parish church when I was a still a girl. Of course, I attended the Baptist church in those days. Since my parents disapproved of me associating with Catholic boys, I barely knew him then. With all of the wonderful twists and turns that life can take, we're now each other's best friends, drinking partners, and confessors. T-LIAM-G!

When Father Cowberries was a boy, he was a mischievous soul and he found easy marks in Martha Mayhem and Priscilla Bunhead. That little rascal played the most outrageous tricks on them. I'll never forget the time that Priscilla came to school with her hair all stuck together.

That little altar boy, whose nickname was Tiger, had been waiting for Priscilla to pass under a tree where he had cleverly hidden himself. When she came strolling along with her rat's nest of hair, he dumped a pot of honey that was mixed with glue right smack on top of her head. By the time she got home, she was screaming bloody murder and her head was covered with flies.

Martha was always attracting trouble and Tiger had a particularly wicked prank in mind for her. He managed to catch her in an orchard with her boyfriend, Crabby Crandall, with their pants down. While the two of them were involved in behavior unbecoming to Baptists, he sneaked behind the crabapple tree where they were doing their thing and he stole their clothes. Too bad for them that there weren't any fig leaves around in that Garden of Eden!

Martha was grounded for the rest of the year and she lost all of her babysitting jobs. That was just fine with Tiger Cowberries. He had grown sick and tired of her yanking his pants down and paddling his butt with his mother's big rubber spatula whenever he'd tried to pull a prank on her. Martha was never allowed to see Crabby again; and, to this day, she holds Father Cowberries responsible for her fate of being an old maid.

Tiger changed his ways after he survived being struck by lightning. Our Baptist minister used him as an example during a sermon when he talked about God getting even with sinners for their wicked ways. Tiger, now the devout Catholic, disagreed. He had seen the light and he believed that God had given him a calling to electrify others to become good Catholics.

At the age of sixteen, he decided he was going to become a priest. I must confess that I developed a secret crush on him after that time. Looking back, I can see where his example may have inspired me to pursue my own vocation as a nun.

Now, let me see! Surely I must have something I should be confessing to Father Cowberries. I think I'll just take a little stroll over to his confessional. I'm sure I'll think of something of which I need to unburden myself. I always feel so relaxed and refreshed after a good confession to Father. He always seems to enjoy it too!

Chapter 8

"*T*-LIAM-G class! This is Sister Mary Olga Fortitude coming to you. Now! Today's lesson in holiness has to do with the Golden Rule. Now really, children, there's no other lesson that's more important in this whole wide world of ours!"

"If you can learn this lesson well, you'll turn out better than most of the adults in this community. Just don't let them in on our little secret. That will be between you, me, and the lamppost. Let's just pretend that the lamppost is Jesus. After all, he is the fairest of them all even though we all know people who are arrogant enough to think that they fill that bill. Well, there's time enough for them to wake up or they might get a nasty little surprise in the end!"

Well, that's how I started out this morning's class. Wouldn't you know it! Little Fartley Dinkledorf caused another uproar. When I asked the class if anyone knew what the Golden Rule meant, Fartley erupted in a burst of laughter. That's when I made the mistake of asking him to answer the question.

He could barely stifle himself when he replied, "Doody unto others as you would have them doody unto you."

Perhaps that's just another way of saying, if you'll pardon the expression, "Shit happens." God knows I get plenty of that from Mother Carmen! As for Fartley, I guess he is just another cross I shall have to bear.

After much soul searching as to how I can reach that irascible child, I've decided to throw caution to the wind so to speak. I began to think about the upcoming Christmas Pageant and I decided to cast him in the role of our blessed Savior. Perhaps, if he portrays the blessed Christ child, he will cast away his inclination to cast his own ill winds within our hallowed community. Well! There's plenty of time to prepare for that since Christmas is still nine months away.

Now! As for my classes in Advanced Holiness for adults, I've had my eye on a certain young lady. I believe she has the potential to help me spread the message that all of us are capable of achieving this state of grace. Her name is Lucy Lovely. She's a beautiful blossoming young woman who loves Jesus as much as I do. Although she is tempted by the ways of this world as we all are, I believe that she may indeed be able to follow in my footsteps.

I must confess that I have an ulterior motive. She's very fond of me and, God knows, I need all of the support I can get within this community. Mother Carmen isn't going any easier on me. She reminds me of the evil stepmother in *Cinderella.* Guess who she's cast in the role of Cinderella?

It's just that I'll never escape Mother's clutches by meeting Prince Charming. Personally, I think that Lucy would be a more fitting princess. Yet, I have my hopes that she will grow weary of this world and seek solace in our own humble convent. She would make a marvelous nun!

I've got my work cut out for me. We don't accept any women in our cloister as new nuns after the age of forty. While I don't know it for a fact, I think that Lucy might be somewhere in her early thirties. There's still time and there's always hope; that is, unless the Baptists get her first!

It's not that there's anything wrong with Baptists. Some of them are even friends of mine; and, my "dear" father, God rest his soul, remained a Baptist until the very end. I just get into a real snit whenever I see any religion casting judgments against any of God's children; and, some of those Baptists do. Of course, there are other denominations, not to mention some Catholics, along with other religions who do the same; but, you didn't hear that from me!

Let's face it, we Christians don't have a monopoly on moral or religious superiority. I just hate it whenever anyone says it's my way or the highway. Personally, I think the High Way is the way to go. Whenever anyone sees the world in just black and white, they end up closing their minds to the mystery of God, as well as to the beauty of nature and of all God's children.

I say, "Stop trying to play God and stop casting your judgments! Enough gloom and doom! God paints nature as well as everyone in the world. He paints us in all the colors of the rainbow, not to mention how he paints each of us with those other differences that makes each of us unique. I say wake up and turn on the color!"

Well now! I guess I missed my calling. I could have been a preacher, but I don't know if any women can be preachers in the Baptist church and I don't care! I'll remain humble and do my own little part for God here at the Have A Heart convent. Let's all remember that we can do our own part to spread the good word around. The good word is that there's a new covenant and that has to do with love and forgiveness. Beyond that, there is only joy and that's what God wants for each and every one of us.

I say, "Lighten up and take it easy. Live and let live. Mind your own business. Don't try to pick the speck out of somebody else's eye unless you take the log out of your own. Judge not, lest ye be judged! To thine own self be true. Make yourself like little children. Then, you may enter the kingdom of heaven, and, that is within each and everyone of us. We are all a part of God."

Oh Lord! I really should have been a preacher! Now! Where was I before I started beating around the bushes again? I say enough Bushes and the likes of him! Oh my God! Maybe I should have become a politician instead. Never mind! Let's just hope and pray that the political climate will become more humane. May God grant us a leader who believes in love instead of fear and judgment.

We just have to remember that there's a bit of good and bad in everything, not to mention in each and everyone of us. Let's just stick to pulling the weeds out of our own garden and let the rest of the world go it's own way. God will sort it all out in the end. Now, isn't that wonderful!

Well now! I've run out of time for today. Besides, my throat is very parched; so, let's all break for refreshments. I hope mine won't be too excruciating! After all, I have to get up at the break of dawn for my morning vigil before I begin a new day with those bright and eager faces of my children.

Chapter 9

T-LIAM-G, my dears! This is Sister Mary Olga Fortitude coming to you. Now! I had another very productive confession with Father Cowberries last night. First, he heard my confession. Then, I heard his.

We were having such a good time; or, should I say such a spiritual time, that we both drained our refreshment bottles. I'll have to see if Randy Cowboy will make a special trip into town to get each of us some of the good stuff. Mum's the word on Father's and my continuing spiritual experiences in the confessional!

I'm sure it's just a coincidence, but I've had a number of parishioners come to me looking for advice. Let's just say that, in each case, these parishioners have unburdened their souls in much the same manner that one would do during a Holy confession. The only difference is that I'm not bound by the seal of the confessional. With that said, I'm sure the Lord won't mind if I tell you some of their stories in order to provide you with spiritual instruction and illumination.

Now! If you can't grasp the finer points, don't feel guilty; not unless you need to! After all, we're all only human and that is what each of these stories certainly demonstrates. Now! If you still can't get the message, don't feel dumber than a box of rocks.

The bottom line is that each of these stories is just plain wacko-hilarious. Now! Isn't that really the truth about life? It's either wacko-funny or somewhere in between; and, how would any of us get through life without humor? Praise God!

Now! I'm sure you haven't forgotten my story about Jules Jesslike Pappas. The one thing about Jules and his family is that there's always a new story unfolding in each of their own lives. Thank God that they trust me enough to confide in me! Their stories provide endless hours of entertainment. Er! I mean that their stories are filled with wonderful lessons in humanity or the lack thereof. Isn't that the truth about the rest of us as well! Come on! Fess up to Sister Mary Olga. Perhaps I can tell your story to the rest of the world some day.

Now! Where was I? Oh yes, how could I ever forget about Jules! Let me start by having a little discussion about the insanity of prejudice. In Jules' case, I'm talking about the evils of racism. Well, let's face it. We're all racists! What on earth are you all muttering about? You heard me right! Every person has a superiority complex and each of us is unnaturally prejudiced.

It's not that we're born that way. We're indoctrinated with a lot of wrong information from the time we're just little babies. We grow up in our comfy cozy or not so comfy cozy worlds, surrounded by people just like us. By the time we're ready to venture out into the world, we're totally programmed by our life experiences. It's our responsibility to unlearn all of the negative messages we have learned during our lives if we're going to follow the High Way to God.

For some peculiar reason we tend to be afraid of people who are different from us. Whenever we're afraid of something or someone, we start right in casting our judgments. Guess what? Life is short and hopefully sweet, but we're all going to die someday. Well, that hits the nail right on the head of the coffin! So, why not live a little in the meantime and open your mind!

Now! Some of you may say I'm dead wrong and you're entitled to your opinions. Let's just say that De-Nile isn't just a river in Egypt! Have you looked in the mirror lately? All you have to do is ask yourself, "Am I prejudiced?" I'll be right around the corner with my camera and I'll take a picture of your expression when you ask yourself that question. The camera doesn't lie and your picture will be worth a thousand words. Guess what? God's got his camera going all the time and he knows every single naughty or nice thought that lurks in your brain. You may be able to fool yourself, but you can't fool God!

That's okay, my children. Jesus understands and forgives you. It isn't easy being human. The thing is, if we don't eat humble pie on a regular basis, we tend to become too full of ourselves and then that devil, the ego takes over. We may become proud and arrogant or we may make excuses while we try to defend our way of thinking. Let's just say we can become self-righteous. Then, our minds close like a steel trap and we comfort ourselves by surrounding ourselves with people who tend to think like us. That keeps us at a safe distance from the people and things we're afraid of.

The things of which we're always most afraid are those parts of ourselves at which we don't want to look. Instead, we distract ourselves with the busy-ness of life and we fill ourselves up with people, places, and things that seem to make us feel better. Guess what? Only God can do that for you! When you close your mind, you are no longer thinking with your heart. When that happens, there's no way for the Holy Spirit to get in with his loving messages. Yet, most of us play this game over and over. Then, we remain locked in the insanity of our delusions.

Good Lord! Here I am on the pulpit again when I was going to tell you a story about Jules. Let's just say that he knows prejudice from the inside out. Unfortunately, the biggest devil in Jules' life is how he takes that on and judges himself. Luckily for him, he can confide in someone such as my humble self.

As long as I allow the Holy Spirit to flow through me, I can be an instrument of God's divine healing, as we all can be. Of course, I enjoy gilding the lily with some other spirits in order to provide a little respite from this crazy world, not to mention the wrath of Mother Carmen Burana!

Now! Where was I? Oh yes! I was going to tell you about Jules' latest challenge. Let's just say that it comes in the form of his paramour. Her name is Lula Mae Bunsaplenty. Lula Mae comes from a long line of Bunsaplentys who were endowed with ample posteriors. In Lula Mae's case, you could set a cafeteria tray on top of her derriere. If it was loaded with food, the problem would be that your meal would be scattered far and wide with the first full swivel of her hips.

Yes, Lula Mae likes her food. That's the way she likes to escape from her problems. Let's just say that her problems, like everyone else's, always catch up with her in the end. Of course in her case, that happens literally; not that Jules minds. He likes a full-figured gal; and, Lula Mae could have given Aunt Jemimah a run for her money before she'd eaten her first thousand pancakes. Still, she would have beat Aunt Jemimah hands down.

Lula Mae keeps saying that she's going to go on a diet like Oprah Winfrey. Unlike Oprah, Lula Mae is a great procrastinator. What's more, she'd never get off the starting line in a marathon unless Kentucky Fried Chicken was being served on the finish line.

Jules has always prided himself on leading a rather vanilla life, despite his chocolate exterior. He's always avoided dating people of his father's race, as he's tried to escape what he considers to be his dark side. How unfortunate! Of course, who am I to judge? Then, again, he never even knew his father. How sad! Perhaps he's just more comfortable with white folks since he grew up in a home with a white mother and two white sisters.

Now! Jules met Lula Mae when he drove Diddles Dinkledorf down to Mississippi to spend Thanksgiving with Diddles' great-niece, Baby Burpee. That's another story about a gal who likes her food. That shall come later.

While Diddles was busy getting acquainted with Baby's fiance, Junior Rathbone, Jules decided to take a stroll through the countryside. Jules has always taken pride in his physique and he has been a strong advocate of exercise. Perhaps, you could even say that he's gone a little bit overboard in that regard. Let's just say that his mode of exercise hasn't been confined to a gym or to his famous cross-country strolls. That should really inspire our elder parishioners since Jules is now an octagenarian.

Yes, my dears, he likes the ladies and he's gotten just as much exercise on a horizontal plane as he has on the vertical one. Folks, I'm trying to exercise some discretion here! After all, Jules is a proud man; and he generally leads an upright life.

Good Lord! I'm still being haunted by that scene down by the old mill stream! Anyhow, Jules is indeed a fine specimen of manhood. Help me, Jesus! Let me just pause so that I may clear my mind of those lurid images by refreshing myself with some holy spirits while I offer up a couple of smoky prayers with my Marlboros.

Ah, that's better! Now! Where was I? Ah yes! Jules was strolling through the lush Mississippi countryside when he came upon a damsel in distress. He happened to notice an extremely curvaceous woman bent over the trunk of her vintage Cadillac. His pulse and his pace quickened as he observed her ample rear end wiggling and jiggling like a bowl full of jelly.

When he arrived on the scene, he noticed that the woman seemed to be stuck in a fascinating position. One of her large breasts was wedged between the car jack which had been carelessly tossed in the middle of a discarded rimless spare tire.

When she became aware of Jules presence, she exclaimed, "Could y'all help me, kahnd suh?"

Like a knight in shining armor, Jules rose to the occasion; in more ways than one, I can assure you! He sidled up to this beauty and she let out an appreciable and appreciated murmur of delight since Jules' big pole was in full bloom.

"Oh mah!" she exclaimed. "Ah hopes Ah hasn't troubled y'all, kahnd suh."

"Why certainly not, Madam!" he exclaimed as he feasted his eyes on her breast which reminded him of a loaf of dark rye bread.

Jules quickly changed his position as he tenderly caressed that voluptuous breast and began to knead it from within the confines of that dirty spare tire. He let out his own exclamation of delight as that beautiful dark brown breast popped out of the confines of Lula Mae's low-slung dress. Ever the gentleman, he said, "Pardon me, Ma'am." Then, he discretely turned away while she deposited her mother load back into her summer frock.

That's when Jules introduced himself to Lula Mae. She expressed her gratitude by inviting him to join her for a picnic. Even though Jules wasn't hungry, how could he refuse such a kind offer? He helped her lift the huge picnic basket she had been trying to reach which was also wedged on the far side of that tire. Lula Mae gathered a colorful blanket and the two of them ambled down to a shady spot by the river for what would be their first date. The rest, as one could say, was another part of his-story.

Well now! The dinner bell is ringing and I mustn't be late. Mother Carmen will only suspect that I've been up to no good if I'm not on time to lead the sisters in grace. Don't worry. I'll finish the story later. T-LIAM-G, my dears!

Chapter 10

T-LIAM-G, my dears! This is Sister Mary Olga Fortitude coming to you. Now! I hope you'll forgive me for the interruption of our story. I've had a little misadventure myself.

Mother Carmen was in a particularly foul mood last night. Mind you, I made it to dinner in time to say grace. Even so, she kept giving me the evil eye throughout our mealtime. When dinner was over, she took me aside and she gave me a lecture on the dangers of expressing opinions that diverged from the positions of Rome.

I thought to myself, "Good Lord, Mother! I'm getting pretty fed up with the Romans! After all, consider what they did to Jesus! Perhaps they've developed a little guilt complex."

I was so grateful to be able to get away from her when the bell rang for evening vespers. I felt so much more at peace afterwards. Of course, I was getting rather thirsty; so, I was most anxious to quench my parched throat and to smoke a pack or two of Marlboros. Since I couldn't think of anything to confess to Father Cowberries - I really wanted to smoke and I couldn't very well get away with that in the confessional – I decided to throw caution to the wind and I visited cubicle number four in the convent bathroom.

As luck would have it, all of the other sisters went directly to their cells following vespers; so, I had the whole place to myself. While I generally refrained from smoking in the lavatory, I was feeling particularly holy and I wanted to offer up prayers in my favorite manner. I also wanted to tie one on!

I opened the bathroom window and I turned on the exhaust fan. Then, I secreted myself in my private potty. I retrieved my bottle of Old Granddad from the toilet tank, settled myself on my well-worn seat, and I prepared to get tanked myself.

I was only halfway through my bottle and my first pack of Marlboros when I heard the lavatory door thrust open with a resounding bang. What a rude awakening from my holy reverie! I stumbled to my feet and I tried to take the lid off the toilet tank, but I lost my balance and I dropped the porcelain top which immediately cracked in two as it made a bigger bang than the one before it. Then, I noticed shards of glass and the remainder of my bourbon spilling out of my stall in a cascading lovely brown slick and onto the bathroom floor. The gig was up and I knew who I'd find on the other side of the cubicle door.

Before I could brace myself to face my own wicked witch of the west, I heard her angry voice echoing throughout the tiled chamber. "Sister Mary OLGA Fortitude!" she exclaimed. "Come out of that toilet immediately!"

I shoved my pack of Marlboros back into my habit before I gathered what was left of my dignity and I prepared to meet my arch nemesis, Mother Carmen Burana. As I tried my best to gracefully exit the toilet stall, I slipped on the remains of Old Granddad and I landed smack dab on my well-padded posterior on that hard tile floor. Fortunately, I had the grace to see the humor in the situation, but Mother Carmen didn't seem to get the joke.

Her face was as crimson as a rouged-up N.B.A.W.

I started to laugh when I thought to myself, "How appropriate!"

Mother Carmen looked like she was about to explode and her voice was as tight as a violin string when she opened her mouth. I had a sense of deja vu when she finally spoke.

"Sister Mary OLGA Fortitude!" she once again exclaimed. "You are a disgrace to the community of the Have A Heart convent! Apparently I haven't been able to get through to you before; so, I'm going to make an example of you to this entire community. If I had it in my power I would strip you of your habit as well as your other vulgar habits. Only God can help you with the latter."

"Of course, I could have you sent away to another community; but, that would only make it too easy on you. I'm going to force you to face your disgrace right here in the bosom of this parish. This shall be your penance. Effective immediately, your classes in Advanced Holiness will be canceled. Since there are no other sisters qualified to teach them, everyone will have to suffer. You will have to live with the guilt of their loss."

Mother Carmen continued with her tirade by saying, "What's more, I am going to make you wish that you were the Blessed Virgin on the road to Calvary. I'm going to search your cell for contraband, even if I have to remove all of the floorboards. Then, you shall remain in solitary confinement in your cell for the next week where you can contemplate the errors of your ways."

"Simple meals will be brought to you and you will have to toilet yourself on a chamber pot. You will not even speak to the nun who will deliver your meals. I will see to it that you are on bended knee from sunup until sundown. Now, before I sequester you, go make a confession to Father Cowberries while I search your cell. I'll have another sister escort you to the confessional to make sure that you don't get away with anything else before this night is through!"

Well, at least her last sentence was music to my ears. Mind you, I had a load to get off my chest with Father Cowberries. Mother Carmen had represented a lifelong challenge to me of trying to find love in my heart for "the enemy." Thank God, she had no idea of what else went on in that confessional!

Father Cowberries was very understanding as well as being a most generous soul. My imminent suffering would be lightened by the two bottles that he supplied which I tied to my bra straps for the long march to my purgatory. Thank God, I had ample room in my over-sized habit; however, my bra straps cut deeply into my flesh on that return trip to my cell. It was a small price to pay for mercy.

My name isn't Fortitude for nothing! I made it through that dark week by the grace of God, along with a little help from Old Granddad. I had two challenges during that long vigil. The first one involved trying to find forgiveness in my heart for Mother Carmen Burana. I'm sure she means well, but I must confess that I've had the most difficult time trying to let go of the lifetime chip I've had on my shoulder concerning her. God forgive me.

The other challenge was having to go cold turkey on my cigarette habit. You can rest assured that I made a beeline to Diddles Dinkledorf as soon as I was freed from my cell. God bless his soul! He'd continued to do his mercy shopping on my behalf while I was in solitary confinement. I took a long and reverent walk after visiting him and I smoked an entire pack of Marlboros while I offered up prayers of gratitude to our Father.

The one advantage to not having smoked in an entire week was that I experienced dizzying rushes of ecstasy during my walk. That led me to wonder if Diddles had played a trick on me and given me some wacky tobaccy. I had to stop and sit at several points since I almost felt as if I was going to topple right over. Of course, my poor knees didn't help. After spending those long days on my knees, they weren't too sure of themselves; but, God gave me the grace to carry on. Praise the Lord!

Well! The lunchtime bell has sounded and I will be teaching my dear children for the first time in a week directly afterwards. Hopefully I can earn back Mother's grace and recommence my classes in Advanced Holiness before too long. T-LIAM-G!

Chapter 11

Now! I was telling you a tale about some misadventures in Mississippi. Well! Jules continued to have his Miss Adventures with Ms. Lula Mae Bunsaplenty. Lula Mae was a free spirit who had chosen to remain single. She wasn't exactly what you'd call a career girl, but she managed to get by in this world by employing her feminine wiles. Mind you, she didn't go about it in the manner in which Mother Carmen had done during her previous "career." Lula Mae considered herself a good girl and she always managed to find herself a new man to provide for her high maintenance needs as soon as her previous affair had come to a dramatic finish.

The only problem was that Lula Mae was starting to get a little "long in the tooth." She'd done a lot of living in her forty-eight years. The well of available prospects in Mississippi was starting to dry up; so, Lula Mae had packed up her Caddy and was going to strike off on a new adventure up north. Jules proved to be an answer to her prayers.

Jules also proved to be an unlikely match for the likes of Lula Mae, but that didn't present any problem for either of them. He was still a very virile and attractive man at the ripe old age of eighty-four. His physical prowess and his genteel ways made him a perfect catch for Lula Mae. She was impressed by his cultured background in addition to his fraternal connection to his famous twin sister. His beautiful cafe au lait complexion also proved to be a feather in her cap as far as the dark-skinned Lula Mae was concerned.

Now! It's not that Jules hadn't dabbled on the other side of the racial fence, but most of his past affairs had been with women of little color. Lula Mae represented a package he'd never considered in his past, but he was up for an adventure. While Diddles was getting acquainted with Baby's new fiance, Junior Rathbone, Jules and Lula Mae got very well-acquainted with each other.

At the end of all of these serendipitous "getting-to-know-you" adventures, Lula Mae had finally pinpointed her new northern destination. She decided to take Jules up on his offer of coming with him for an extended visit in our heavenly haven of Bucksnort. So, Jules made the return trip in Lula Mae's commodious Cadillac, leaving Diddles to drive home alone.

God only knows the trouble that Diddles might get into on the return trip, but that's another story. In the meantime, Diddles spent a memorable Thanksgiving week with Baby Burpee and Junior.

Baby and Junior had one thing in common. They both liked their food. The two of them could polish off a barbecued turkey in one sitting. After having a meal with all of the trimmings, they'd each share a shoefly pie and still be ready for a bedtime snack a couple of hours later.

Baby had met Junior down at the local swimming hole on a sultry July evening and it was love at first sight. It was a bright moonlit night when Junior ambled down the path to the river for the only form of exercise that he had ever enjoyed. He couldn't believe his luck when he saw another full moon illuminated by the light of the silvery moon.

There, in the refreshing waters of the Mississippi, was a goddess of grand girth. She was doing the breast stroke with her own melon-sized mammaries swaying in her wake like the wings of an angel. Her bleached blond hair looked like strands of liquid silver; but, to Junior's grateful eyes, it was pure gold.

Junior let out a whoop and he quickly shed his clothes. Then, he took a running dash onto a tree trunk that had fallen into the Mississippi. As he began his take off from the tree trunk, that tree reverberated with shock waves that echoed a refrain with the bouncing bounty of his heaving buttocks. He leaped into those previously cool waters with a splash almost as big as the time that old cypress tree had toppled into the river.

Baby stopped in mid-stroke and she struggled against the current that her ample body had been creating in order to turn toward the resounding splat on those previously still waters. At first, she couldn't see a thing except the approaching wake of the spreading circle of waves that Junior had created. Then, she let out a delighted gasp of surprise when she saw the beaming smile on Junior's porcine face as it emerged from the water in the midst of the encroaching waves. Not even the resistance of the water could slow the momentum of Junior's approach and he came to a final rest with his face gently nestled between Baby's billowing breasts.

Never having even kissed a girl before, Junior couldn't believe his luck that Baby didn't push him away. Instead, she gave him a great big hug and she kissed him right on the lips. He let out a grateful cry of "Baby!"

She responded by saying, "How'd y'all know mah name, big guy?"

He simply looked back at her with a grin that made his face as big and round as the moon above. That was the start of a romance made in heaven.

Neither Baby nor Junior had ever had a romance before and it didn't take long for Junior to pop the question. Baby was so excited, she wanted to let the whole world know. Her mama was delighted, but poor Baby's father was in heaven. Bless his soul.

Baby's next closest father figure was her Great Uncle Diddles. As soon as Junior had proposed to Baby, she had called up her Uncle Diddles and she'd asked him if he would give her away. Diddles, in the role of Daddy, had told her that he must first meet the young man; so, he then made arrangements to visit them that Thanksgiving.

Little did Diddles know what a marvelous cook Baby had turned out to be. Her fiance', Junior, was no slouch in that department either. That was part of the glue that brought the two of them together. They just loved to spend their time cooking in the kitchen.

It's a good thing they knew how to whip up a lot of food while they were at it or they'd never have been able to manage to get dinner on the table. They practically ate a whole meal while they were cooking. Even so, they still had big appetites when dinner was served; and, as new lovebirds, they had developed another appetite that led to a new form of exercise. This helped them make room for a big dessert after flailing the mounds of their voluptuous bodies about on Baby's buoyant water bed.

Now! Mind you, I've had to come a long way in my views on sex. You'll have to remember that I entered the convent in those dark days before Vatican II. It's not that the Roman Catholic church has changed their positions on the shame of premarital sex or sexual relations that aren't for the purpose of procreating future servants to Rome. As a lifelong virgin, I have no direct experience in these matters; so, how am I in any position to judge what is good or healthy behavior? Then, I've had my own prejudices to deal with, especially those connected to Mother Carmen's notorious past.

With that said, I think that it's important that we all look within our hearts concerning these delicate matters. Whatever ideas have been put into our heads that have to do with guilt and shame are only damaging to our souls. Only God can truly judge each and every one of us; and, God is really about love as Jesus has taught us. As long as we are light-hearted, respectful, and loving in all of our relations with others, what can be the harm? So, I'm going to go out on a limb when I say that I believe these same rules should be applied to sex.

Any other judgments that are made about the loving intimacy between two people are wrong. It's nobody's business what happens between two people if they're not hurting each other or anyone else. We must all be careful with our thoughts and words. How can we judge anyone's experience without walking a mile in their shoes? Let us remember that God gave us two ears and one mouth. It's a lot easier in the end, if we hold our tongue about things that don't involve us rather than it is to eat our own words.

Lord, here I am on the pulpit again! Well, it's time for evening vespers, so I'd better finish my tales another day. T-LIAM-G!

Chapter 12

T-LIAM-G, my dears! This is Sister Mary Olga Fortitude coming to you. Now! A most disturbing situation has been developing within our parish. Surely you remember me telling you about Priscilla Bunhead. That unfortunate woman seems to be the culprit in this particular case. She has spearheaded a most conservative and judgmental organization and she is playing the pied piper to many of the vulnerable female souls in our parish.

Priscilla, like myself, has been a teacher for all of her adult life. She is a high school home economics teacher and she also teaches a course in proper grooming and etiquette for young ladies. She basically follows in the tradition of Amy Vanderbilt; and, we all know what happened to her! Priscilla's own etiquette course flew out the window during the 1960's, but it has regained favor during these conservative times.

The course has become so popular that she's even offering it as an adult education class. In my opinion, she is trying to seduce my female students of Advanced Holiness into practicing shallow worldly values instead of becoming who they are truly meant to be. She's even getting her evil clutches upon my dear Lucy Lovely. What I'm really concerned about is the influence she has been exerting upon impressionable young female minds.

Priscilla is facing mandatory retirement this year and she has stepped up her campaign. She's even formed an auxiliary group called B.U.N. That acronym stands for Bunheads Unite Now. All of her converts have adopted the habit of wearing their hair in tight little buns.

Mind you, Priscilla doesn't have any alternative to that particular hairstyle. That is the result of her former teenage habit of abusing her hair, not to mention the honey and glue pot incident. As I see it, the problem is that she's trying to force her values upon others in order to make herself feel good about herself. That is what I would call a control freak; but, you didn't hear that from me!

I've been watching this situation develop with increasing alarm. Her students and followers seem to have lost all sense of individuality as they have adopted Priscilla's conservative agenda. I'm sure that the practice of wearing their hair in tight little buns does nothing to enhance the ability of their constricted little heads to think independently. I believe she is brainwashing our youth along with other young women in the community. I can only shudder to think where this may lead. We must remember that vanity is one of the seven deadly sins.

My greatest disappointment was when she seduced my own protegee, the lucky Lucy Lovely. Almost overnight, Lucy changed from her habit of wearing her long, golden tresses in a beautifully flowing style into that of wearing a tight little bun on the back of her head.

Lord, have mercy! Every day, more and more young girls and women are appearing in our community with those tight little buns. It's almost as frightening a phenomenon as what happened in *The Stepford Wives*. God only knows what Priscilla's ultimate agenda is, but I shall keep a close eye on her.

For once in my life, I must say that I'm indebted to Martha Mayhem. Martha and Priscilla have never seen eye to eye. Martha's been hanging onto a grudge with Priscilla that approaches the magnitude of the grudge she has against Father Cowberries. It wasn't long after the incident when the young Tiger Cowberries had caught Martha in a compromising position when this new feud began.

While Martha was grounded by her parents those many years ago, Priscilla started parading by Crabby Crandall's orchard every day. The boy eventually succumbed to her charms, but prim and proper Priscilla didn't allow Crabby the goodies that Martha had so freely dispensed. Nevertheless, when the time came for the senior prom, Priscilla proudly marched on Crabby Crandall's arm while Martha had to stay home and stew more than just tomatoes. Crabby eventually got tired of Priscilla's prissiness, but Martha got even.

One summer's eve, when Martha's parents had finally let her out on parole, she got her revenge. Martha knew Priscilla's most closely guarded secret. Priscilla was flat-chested, though she carefully disguised that situation by stuffing her bra with wads of toilet paper. To the unsuspecting world, Priscilla paraded around town with a bust line that would have made Marilyn Monroe envious. Martha decided it was time to take her down a peg or two and expose the pegs that Priscilla had been masquerading as a pair of hooters.

Martha also knew some of Priscilla's other habits which led her to hatch a brainstorm. Priscilla's family was the only one in the community that owned an in-ground swimming pool. What's more, prissy Priscilla enjoyed skinny dipping after her parents had gone to bed. I'm not going go so far as to suggest that she developed this habit after she discovered the joys of the pool's jacuzzi. That's none of my business; however, Martha knew better.

Martha told several of the community's teenage boys that she knew a way for them to get a first-hand look at Priscilla's pom poms. She also suggested that they might even get more of a show than just Priscilla's bouncing boobies. She invited them to come on over to Priscilla's home and hide behind the bushes just before the appointed hour of Prissy's poolside frolic. Every boy showed up on cue; and, soon thereafter, so did Priscilla.

It was a dark night and the boys were getting restless when they heard Priscilla take her plunge. Martha waited until Priscilla had "assumed the position" in the pool's jacuzzi. As Priscilla was entertaining herself with those jacuzzi jets, Martha tiptoed to the back of the house and threw on the switch that turned on the floodlights.

Priscilla was suddenly illuminated in all of her glory, but she didn't have the glorious goods of which the boys had been dreaming since they'd hit puberty. Priscilla let out a loud shriek and she went running into her house like a drowned rat; pun intended! Martha had the last laugh and it didn't stop until she got home.

Moving forward in time nearly fifty years, Martha decided it was time to take the proud and prissy Priscilla down another peg or two, though this time Martha had her eyes on another prize. She had become sick and tired of seeing so many young girls and women in the community parading around wearing the same buns that reminded her of Priscilla.

She decided that enough was enough when her sisters, her niece, and her great- niece adopted Priscilla's prissy hair fashion. In no uncertain terms, she told her nieces that they'd better listen to Aunt Martha and get rid of their buns before she took matters into her own hands. With that said, Martha knew exactly how she was going to deal with proud and prissy Priscilla.

Martha became a surprise guest at one of Prissy's Bunheads Unite Now rallies. You'd think that she would have stood out like a sore thumb with her own unkempt and flyaway hair among that sea of Prissy's bunheads, especially as she approached the podium where Priscilla was rallying her troops.

No one seemed to notice that Martha had one hand behind her back until it was too late. A collective gasp went up from the audience as Martha produced a set of pruning sheers and promptly chopped off Priscilla's bun. Once again, Priscilla went off screaming into the night while Martha held up that bun as if it was Marie Antoinette's head after the guillotine had sliced it right off.

Now class! I don't condone violence, but that just goes to show you where false pride can lead one. Still, it always helps to have a sense of humor about these situations. I just can't help but think of the time when I pulled the hair out of Priscilla's little dolly. I certainly can understand why Martha was just as pleased as punch. Speaking of refreshments, my throat is getting rather parched. I think this would be a fitting time for a break while I fortify myself with some, shall we say, heavenly spirits.

Chapter 13

"*N*ow class! I think I've just scored another one for God's team; and, if I don't mind saying so myself, for Sister Mary Olga Fortitude. Will you all make note of Lucy Lovely. During our refreshment break, she's taken off her bun-holder and has let her lovely tresses down just like Rapunzel. I hope I'm not embarrassing you, my dear. I gather that you took a hint when I told the story about Martha Mayhem's latest revenge."

"As the rest of you may not know, lucky Lucy hasn't been so lucky when it's come to receiving phone calls from Martha. For some odd reason, Martha has taken a dislike to Lucy and has been very abusive in the phone messages that she's left for her. I guess that just shows what a bully and a coward that Martha actually is. Even so, poor Martha likes to think that no one messes with Martha without getting a good dose of mayhem!"

"Now! Not that I'm trying to single anyone out, but I'm going to take this opportunity to make a pitch for all of you single gals to consider the idea of taking a new groom to replace your fantasies. I'm talking about our Savior, Jesus Christ. It would be such an honor to God, as well as a feather in my cap, if you'd decide to join the Have A Heart Convent and become a bride of Christ. Excuse me for just a minute, class."

"Where are you going, Lucy Lovely? Class isn't over yet! What's that, my dear? I certainly didn't teach you those expressions in our classes on Advanced Holiness! You must be traumatized and be reliving memories of those phone messages from Martha Mayhem. I'll just assume you're reciting one of her unpleasant remarks to you."

"Well class, I hope we haven't lost her. After all, these are trying times and we need all the teachers we can get to carry the message and teach others the ways to Advanced Holiness. I'm sure that Lucy Lovely will gather her senses now that her temples aren't being squeezed within a vice by having her hair pulled tighter than the strings on a banjo. Yes, my dear Lucy will be back; all in good time, my lovely."

I guess it's high time that I get honest about something else. We are in desperate need of new nuns at the convent. We just lost another one of our sisters to the great beyond and none of the rest of us is getting any younger. Yet, God is good and He never gives us any more than we can handle.

I am happy to report that we do have a new sister at the convent, though new is perhaps not the most appropriate way to describe her. Her name is Sister Daniella Shakesalot and she is ninety-five years-old. God bless her soul! You could also say, "Score one for our side." She's a convert from a Shaker Community.

Sister Daniella was the last surviving Shaker of her former community. She is a free spirit with an optimistic zest for life and she'd been looking for another way to serve the Lord. We are most grateful that her search for a new community to join has led her to us. In keeping with her rich background of tradition, she brings the most unorthodox habits to our little parish and she's really shaking things up in a most interesting manner. Our chapel masses have never been the same since she has come into our fold.

When the Holy Spirit comes upon our new sister, she moves us all in the most mysterious ways. As soon as we begin to sing a hymn, she totters from her pew and she suddenly starts to dance. My Lord, you'd never guess her age when she begins swaying with the spirit of her younger years. I must confess that she's moved me and several of the other sisters to join her in her ways of celebrating the Lord.

Suddenly, we are transported to our mass wedding with Our Lord and Savior. Once again, the wedding reception begins when we all dance our first dance with our beloved joint groom, Jesus.

Mother Carmen was noticeably alarmed the first time she witnessed this behavior. Fortunately, she's deferred to the older sister's age and she has indulged her in her habits; but, she hasn't been particularly happy to see some of us other sisters following her ways. Only time will tell if Mother Carmen decides to put the damper on our own moving celebration of the dance.

I'm sharing this story as an example of how important it is to keep an open mind instead of casting judgments against those who are different from us. When we can suspend those judgments, we begin to allow God to grant us new perspectives. As a result, we can come to new understandings about people from different backgrounds and with different beliefs than our own.

If we open our eyes and truly see that they are children of God as well as we are, we begin to embrace our larger humanity. God knows, it is a challenge, but the rewards are great and they will only serve to transform us on the High Way to God. Praise the Lord from whom all blessings flow!

"Now! Where was I? Oh, thank you, God! Lucky Lucy

Lovely has seen the error of her ways and has returned to our fold."

"I hope I'm not embarrassing you, my dear. After all, you are one of my most promising pupils. I'm counting on you to carry the torch of freedom to illuminate the masses of those whose eyes have not yet been truly opened."

"Well, the truth is that God wants us to celebrate! He wants us to celebrate every moment of our lives. With that said, I think it would be a lovely time to break for our own form of celebration. Amanda Ann Adult has prepared the most lovely refreshments for us all."

"I strongly recommend the punch. Let me assure you that it, indeed, packs quite a punch; but, please don't let Mother Carmen know! If you start to sway and dance, just pretend that you are following in the example of Sister Daniella, our resident Shaker. T-LIAM-G!"

"Now, Lucy Lovely, perhaps you'd like to join me outside in the garden. I'm feeling the need to pray and I would welcome your support. Let us remember that all it takes is for two to pray in the name of Jesus. Then, anything, including pure miracles, can occur. These are trying times. The world, as we know it, is going to hell in a hand basket!"

"Now! I'd suggest that we offer up our most fervent prayers in my favorite tradition, accompanied by smoke signals. Don't worry, my dear! No one will see you. It will be our own little secret with God. Besides, I've got plenty of extra Marlboros. Randy Cowboy's been playing Cowboys and Indians again. He just returned from the Indian Reservation with a bounty of Marlboros; but, let's just call them prayer sticks instead."

Chapter 14

T-LIAM-G, my dears! This is Sister Mary Olga Fortitude coming to you. Now! I'm sure you're all wondering about Jules Jesslike Pappas and his new lady love, Lula Mae Bunsaplenty.

We left them in about the same place where they had met. You see, their picnic turned into another type of feast after they polished off Lula Mae's fried chicken, barbecued ribs, potato and macaroni salads, collard greens with pig's feet, black eyed peas, and sweet potato pie. On a blanket, right down there by the river, expresso embraced cafe au lait. The rest would become a continuing part of his-story; and, her-story too!

Well! I guess you know what happened next. Serendipity became their middle names. The two of them piled into Lula Mae's commodious Caddy and they set their compass for their destination of Bucksnort, Wisconsin. Lula Mae pushed the pedal to the metal and they were off on an adventure.

Meanwhile, Diddles Dinkledorf was spending some solitary time singing *Blue Bayou*. As fond as he'd become of Mark Mayhem, he'd found himself increasingly frustrated with the furtiveness of their fondlings. Now that his wife, Babbetina Dinkledorf, had passed into the great beyond, he longed to find a lasting happiness for himself.

As Diddles observed the blossoming love of his great-niece Baby and her fiance', Junior Rathbone, he realized that he had never really had a satisfying love in his life. Then, it hit him with a vengeance. He had always loved Mark Mayhem, but he'd never really been able to allow himself the freedom to let Mark know that.

Diddles suddenly felt a burning desire to call Mark and let him know of his true feelings; but then, he got scared. Mark had made it clear to Diddles that the only thing he wanted from Diddles was a diddling whenever they had had the opportunity. Mark had never ceased to remind Diddles that he was straight as an arrow and that he never wanted his wife, Marjorine, to know about their clandestine affair.

Diddles was overcome with a sense of abiding sadness. Fortunately for Diddles, he was a very practical man and he realized that there was no purpose to be served by staying stuck in his well of grief. That's when he saw the light. He could be free if he wanted to be; and, he didn't have to worry about the judgment of Mark or his sisters way down here in the deep south. So, he grabbed hold of his lifeline and he decided to alter his course. He decided to throw caution to the wind and cast off the shackles of his self-imposed prison of denial. He was going to have his own adventure!

Diddles decided to take a side trip to the Big Easy and take a walk on the wild side in New Orleans. He spruced himself up, he jumped into his 1979 Chrysler Cordoba, and he sailed off into the sunset for what would be only his second night in a big city. Diddles had picked the right city to drive "homo" the point that there was nothing wrong with his being gay.

He parked in the French Quarter and he started off on foot, taking in the timeless architecture of those grand buildings which were set against the backdrop of the lush atmosphere of the city. He felt like Alice in Wonderland as he strolled along the nighttime streets lined with bar after bar. Not knowing that many of these establishments were indeed gay bars, he finally took a chance on a place called The Big Easy Pub.

If nothing else, it reminded him of yours truly, given all of the trips he'd made to fetch my own stash of Old Granddad. Besides, he certainly knew that I wasn't about to pass judgment on his life choices. We'd had many spiritual conferences over the years and I had long ago let him off the hook with my earlier attempts at blackmailing him over his secret affair with Mark Mayhem.

As soon as Diddles entered the dim light of the pub, he walked right up to the long mahogany bar and he sidled up to an attractive Creole man. The man appeared to be about sixty years old and Diddles, at seventy, thought he might stand a chance with him. Before he could open his mouth to make an introduction, the other man spoke to him. In a deep and resonant voice that seemed as if it was dripping with honey, the man asked Diddles if he could buy him a drink. Diddles grinned back at him with a shit-eating grin, if you'll pardon the expression. He'd found himself in the right place where he could finally meet some kindred spirits.

Well! Diddles got into an animated discussion with this man whose name was Francois. The two of them took turns buying each other drinks until Diddles head began to spin. That's when Francois suggested they go dancing.

Well! That brought Diddles up short. He'd never even considered the possibility of dancing with another man unless he brought the other man up short from behind while taking a bow before him.

Off the two of them went, as they tottered onto the sidewalk on that balmy late November evening. They strolled arm and arm to what would be a trip to the land of Oz for Diddles. They walked into another bar which was a discotheque named Over The Rainbow. Diddles started to get dizzy from the sound of the pounding music and flashing lights that were emanating from within this land of Oz. He felt as if every organ in his body was vibrating. At least that let him know that he hadn't died and gone over the rainbow.

The thing that immediately confused Diddles was that there were a small number of women who reminded him of the streetwalkers he'd encountered on his first trip to the Big City in the 1950's. Francois walked right up to one of these garishly painted ladies and he planted a big kiss on her cheek with his own set of full lips. Then, he turned to Diddles and he made the introduction.

When he had been properly introduced to the lady named Jezebel, Diddles behaved like a gentleman and said, "Pleased to meet you, Ma'am."

That's when Jezebel let out a full-throated laugh that echoed with all the depth of a baritone from the Metropolitan Opera. Diddles was momentarily confused. Then he realized his mistake. This was no lady! This was a drag queen.

Well! The night had just begun; and, once the night was through, Diddles would have received an entire education. He couldn't believe the bazoombas that the deep-throated Jezebel was sporting.

He also couldn't believe it when he was in the arms of his new knight in shining armor, Francois. That big surprise came when he later visited Francois' garden district home. There, in the cavern of Francois' eighteenth-century family homestead's master bedroom, Diddles finally found out what it felt like to get diddled himself.

Francois was a gentle lover which was a good thing since he came very well-appointed for the task. Diddles found himself beginning to wonder if he had, indeed, died and gone to heaven. He'd never known such ecstasy in his entire life. He decided he must be in love and he had no qualms letting Francois know his feelings. Fortunately, Francois was a man of great tact at a time when he could have burst Diddles' bubble.

Francois advised Diddles that he wasn't in love. He gently suggested that perhaps Diddles had just made love for the first time in his life. Naturally, Diddles was disappointed with his response, but the chord rang true. Yes, Diddles had made love, but he remembered that there was another man back home whom he truly loved; and, he hoped that someday he'd be able to make love with Mark as he had done with Francois.

Chapter 15

*D*iddles spent a passionate night with Francois and then he, somewhat reluctantly, returned to Baby's home. Having been awake for nearly twenty-four hours, he was ready for the sleep of the dead. He staggered into Baby's downstairs den where he promptly passed out in her Sears sleeper sofa.

Meanwhile, Baby Burpee and Junior Rathbone were having their own marathon night of sweet passion. It was the five-month anniversary of their meeting.

They had developed a tradition for celebrating the passing of each month since their serendipitous first date. It was always right around the time of the next full moon. Then, Baby Burpee would take a moonlit stroll down to the river where she would cast off her 3X-summer frock and take a plunge into the Mississippi.

Again on this evening, Junior Rathbone stood at attention in more ways than one on that riverbank. There, he bared his bouncing, buttocked booty to the light of the silvery moon. Taking a deep breath, he raced forward toward the tree that had fallen into the river where he made a thunderous reverberation as he stomped onto that tree trunk.

With one final and resounding stomp, Junior took a

plunge that sent waves rolling to the other riverbank of the wide Mississippi. Baby let out an exclamation of delight as Junior's billowing form emerged from the deep. Then, the two of them frolicked in the refreshing waters before taking a romantic stroll back to Baby's bedroom.

Baby and Junior had fallen asleep in the wee hours of the morning. The sound of Diddle's approaching classic Cordoba stirred Baby out of her peaceful slumber. That's when she took in the pleasing contours of Junior grandiose girth and she decided that she wanted a turn in the driver's seat herself.

Despite their long night of lovemaking, Baby had an insatiable appetite. There was only thing that was more tempting than a leftover turkey drumstick. That was the soothing sensation of her over-sized water bed, rocking and rolling with warm, pulsating waves while she rocked away during her more intimate delight with Junior.

Baby considered her approach. The full wave effect of her water bed required some careful calculations. Even though Baby wasn't too swift when it came to the subject of physics, she was always willing to take a risk when it came to fulfilling her physical desires. She decided she was going to be an adventuress. She wanted to be able to launch herself onto Junior's trunk in a similar manner to Junior's approach on the fallen tree trunk, down by the river.

She overcame inertia, as she pushed her mammoth form away from Junior in her struggle to get off that water bed. Then, she surveyed the room. That's when she had a brainstorm. She happened to notice the heavy-duty jogging trampoline that she'd bought when she'd last gone on a diet. It was stashed away unceremoniously, and almost forgotten, in her bedroom closet. She placed it at the foot of the bed and she climbed on top of the trampoline.

Then, she took a deep breath and she began to bounce.

With each successive bounce, Baby was lifted higher into the air as she let out giggles of anticipation. Bouncing ever higher, she prepared for her final assault. With all the momentum that those three hundred pounds of Baby could provide, she finally launched her bounty onto the padded frame of the bed. Without skipping a beat, her next bounce would land her right on her target. As she made her final approach to Junior's outstretched corpulence, she raised her knees high and let out a high-pitched "Whee!"

Not one second later, Junior let out a resounding whoop, as Baby crash-landed right on target. At the same time as she landed, a tidal wave began to form within Baby's gigantic water bed. Then, all motion ceased and Baby suddenly realized why she had failed physics.

Before the wave could propel Baby and Junior into new heights of ecstasy, their combined six hundred sixty-six pounds of coupled flesh broke through the durable membrane of the mattress. The bed's frame snapped in two as Baby and Junior hit the floor, while the waves of water splattered over the edge of the bed with a force of pure nature.

Sleeping below them, Diddles was having a vivid dream. One minute he was dreaming about Jezebel's bouncing bozoombas and a moment later he was preparing to enter the baptismal tank at the Bucksnort Baptist Church. That was the very moment that he was roused into reality as the deluge of water started streaming through the floorboards of Baby's bedroom located directly above him.

Well now! Diddles' holiday was over and it was time for him to get back to his job at the Have A Heart Convent. Since Diddles was far from old-fashioned, Junior Rathbone passed the test as a prospective groom for Baby. Diddles didn't even mind the unexpected bridal shower that had rained down upon him on that sultry Mississippi morning.

So, Diddles kissed Baby goodbye and he promised to be back for her marriage to Junior Rathbone. Their wedding was scheduled to take place on the one year anniversary of their meeting, the Fourth of July. Baby and Junior waved their goodbyes and Diddles put the pedal to the metal of his Chrysler Cordoba. Then, he was off in a whirl of dust.

Chapter 16

T-LIAM-G, my dears! This is Sister Mary Olga Fortitude coming to you. Now! I'm sharing these rather intimate tales about some of our parishioners for the purpose of enlightening you, not to titillate you. If you think I'm obsessed with sex, you've got it wrong. I say, "Look in the mirror and see who's the one who is obsessed!"

Granted, I've had my weak moments, but I've become very comfortable within my chaste role. The problem, as I see it, is that too many people take physical intimacy far too seriously. After all, God has a wonderful sense of humor and, if you can't see the humor of being human, you might as well have not even come along for the ride of life.

We're supposed to be here to experience joy. That's where we need to take a lesson from the little children. They are about pure joy. Guess what folks? God placed children in our lives to teach us a lesson, not vice versa. So, put away your fake adult personae and get with the program! Life is all too short; and, hopefully it will be sweet for you too. With all its inevitable pain, it's all the more important to find your pathway to happiness wherever and however you can, as long as you don't hurt anyone in the process.

Now! I'd better back up just a bit and tell you the story about the Mayhem family. You know a little something about Martha and Mark, but did you remember that they have two other sisters? I guess it's pretty obvious that Martha is the black sheep of the family, even though Mark has taken on that judgment of himself. That's just because he doesn't accept his true nature. Well, the consequence of that is that he lives a sneaky life that causes him continual guilt and shame. Now, that really is a shame!

Martha, on the other hand, had some promise as a young girl. She was a rambunctious girl, but she couldn't seem to get past blaming other people for her problems. She eventually wove a web around herself that was filled with resentments and the delusion that other people were out to get her.

I pray that some day she'll wake up and smell the coffee. If only she'd use her high-spiritedness for good instead of dwelling on ways to get even with people, she'd make a marvelous example for other people who've gotten stuck in the victim trap. Even so, she makes a wonderful example of what not to do for you students of Advanced Holiness.

Martha was always jealous of her other sisters. Whenever Mildred earned their parents' favor, Martha claimed it was because Mildred was the prettiest girl. Whenever little Myrtle scored some brownie points, Martha said it was because she was the youngest. That left Martha with another bone to chew regarding her brother, Mark. Martha would always say that he got special attention because he was the only boy. I guess you could say that Martha boxed herself into a corner with no way out. Guess what? That's exactly how her life has turned out for her. Perhaps it's time for her to grow up, but she'll have to discover that for herself.

Mildred married Maynard Mayflower when she was

twenty-one. Maynard was the most eligible bachelor in our parish at the age of thirty-nine. He was also the wealthiest man in town. Unfortunately, he died of a heart attack on their wedding night. The good fortune about her bad fortune was that he left her a couple of bundles. The first bundle was his family's fortune. The second bundle was a baby girl who was born nine months to the day after Maynard was buried in the parish cemetery.

Mildred asked her youngest sister, Myrtle, to be the godmother which only gave Martha another axe to grind. When that baby girl popped out of Mildred, she had the most adorable dimples; so, "Dimples" became her name. Mildred's status as a young and rich widow made her an attractive catch, but Mildred wasn't going to play that game. From the moment she looked into Dimples eyes, she made the decision that no other man was going to come between her and her baby.

Well! Let's just say that Dimples got a lot of attention and was also spoiled very quickly. Nothing but the best was good enough for Dimples. With the passing of each Christmas and birthday, Dimples became the envy of every other little child in the parish. She received the most extravagant gifts and she even got a pony for her sixth birthday. Little Dimples would get dressed up in her Dale Evans cowgirl outfit and ride that pony all over town.

The other children would beg her for a ride, but Dimples would say, "Let your parents buy you your own pony!" It didn't matter to her that none of the other children's parents could afford to do so.

Dimples was frequently excused from her classes so that she could travel to exotic places all over the world. When she'd return to class, she'd always give a show-and-tell presentation that left the other children green with envy.

It was lucky for Dimples that her mother invited all of

the children to accompany them on Dimple's seventh birthday to Disneyland. I must confess that I planted that seed with Mildred since I was concerned that Dimples wouldn't have a friend in this world if she kept on flaunting her goodies in front of the other children. Wouldn't you know it, even Martha was jealous of Dimples!

Now! Mark Mayhem had already married Marjorine Buttersworth before Mildred became married. Finally, Myrtle got married to Milton Merriweather seven years after Mildred had become a sudden widow. This left Martha on the outside, looking in at all of her married siblings. Martha never had another boyfriend after Crabby Crandall.

Both Mark and Myrtle had three children apiece. Then, both of them asked Mildred to become their children's godmother. They wanted their kids to have some of the same privileges as those belonging to their spoiled rotten niece, Dimples. That only served to make Martha feel like even more of an outsider. It wasn't long before Martha wasn't speaking to anyone in her family. Poor Martha!

Well, life went on and the Mayflower and Merriweather children grew up after having been exposed to my own good influence, I must add. Mildred never did remarry, but she did become an important patron of our parish after she, along with her domineering mother-in-law, had royally spoiled little Dimples. Little Dimples left our parish, much to her mother's chagrin. The last I heard was that she was now living on the French Riviera with husband number four, along with her own little Dimples II.

Myrtle led a humble life and tried to be a good godmother to little Dimples, but that had been of little use for that spoiled brat. Mildred saw that all of her nieces and nephews had the best advantages that money could buy.

From that standpoint, I suppose you could say she was a good godmother. Money can't buy everything and, wouldn't you know it, Mark Mayhem's children proved to be a handful.

Myrtle's children all remained in the area and became upright members of our local parish church. All of them married and had children who are now students at the Have A Heart Academy. Mark's children also remained in the area. Let's just say that they had some issues and we'll leave it at that for now.

Now! I was originally speaking about the joy that little children naturally bring into this world. Isn't it amazing how soon that joy can be corrupted for so many? What a shame! Dimples Mayflower is a good example of that, but I'll get to her later on. What I'm dealing with now are the legacies passed on by the families of my current crop of children.

I teach children classes in holiness, modeled on the Have A Heart concept of what would Jesus do? Some of my most promising students are the grandchildren of Myrtle Merriweather. Some of my biggest challenges are the grandchildren of Mark Mayhem and Diddles Dinkledorf. Go figure!

As I've said before, I suppose one could look at it as a matter of the sins of the fathers being passed down to the sons. I prefer to think of it as a matter of improper programming which is modeled by parents of extremely dysfunctional families. Granted, all families are dysfunctional to some degree. We wouldn't be human if we were perfect.

I try to lay down a foundation of good principles of holy living to which all children can aspire. Some make it and some do not. That's just the way of the world.

Good Lord! It's time for evening vespers already. I only hope I'll have a brief chance to fortify myself with a smoky prayer, chased down by Old Granddad. I am definitely going to have to make a confession to Father Cowberries this evening! That will give me an opportunity to wash away the cares of the world in more ways than one. T-LIAM-G!

Chapter 17

*N*ow! Today, I received a call from Amanda Ann Adult. Priscilla Bunhead, one of Jules Jesslike Pappas' next-door neighbors, called her this morning. She advised Amanda Ann that she was concerned about Jules. Priscilla had been massaging her scalp in front of her bedroom window in the middle of the night when she noticed a strange vehicle pull into Jules' driveway.

Priscilla had parted her curtains and she peered out to determine exactly what was going on at her neighbor's home. She was amazed when she saw Jules get out of the car along with a rather broad-in-the-beam and buxom, younger woman of a deep ebony color. Priscilla got out her spyglass and noticed that the maroon Cadillac bore Mississippi license plates.

Her next thought was, "There goes the neighborhood!" She was convinced that the younger woman was an adventuress. She thought Amanda Ann should be aware that someone might be up to no good with her older brother.

At the same time that Priscilla Bunhead had been spying on her neighbor, Jules, her other next-door neighbor, Martha Mayhem, was out in her backyard performing a ritual. She had built a large bonfire and she was preparing to ceremoniously burn the beheaded bun of Priscilla's now-bunless head.

Martha also noticed the strange car pull into her neighbor's drive. Just as Priscilla's bun was sizzling away on the ash heap, Martha's delight turned to vexation when she heard the loud and flamboyant southern drawl of Lula Mae. Martha couldn't stand anyone who was louder than herself and she was not amused.

Meanwhile, across the street, a very old man was taking out his false teeth when he noticed that Caddy pull into his neighbor's driveway. His name was Poopsy Dinkledorf. He was the oldest-surviving patriarch of the Dinkledorf clan.

Poopsy was one hundred-five years-old and he had outlived his wife, Daisy, and one of his children. Only his son, Diddles, and his daughter, Doodums were still alive. Poopsy was rather concerned when he saw Jules get out of that car with the out-of-state license plates. After all, Jules had gone to Mississippi with his son. That caused him to wonder what had become of Diddles.

Poopsy quickly forgot about the whereabouts of his son, when he saw the voluptuous Lula Mae get out of the car. He drew near to his window and he watched her bouncing form as she sashayed up the sidewalk leading to Jules' front door. Poopsy, like Jules, was every bit the lady's man. He didn't care what flavor or color they came in, as long as they had curves in all of the right places.

Now! Let me get back to my phone call from Amanda Ann. I could tell that Amanda Ann was enjoying her early morning Bloody Mary; not that there's anything wrong with that! I, too, had just had a refreshing confession with Father Cowberries. Anyhow, Priscilla Bunhead had suggested to Amanda Ann that she call me to have me check out the situation.

Well now! Considering the source of Amanda Ann's concern, I was careful not to fuel the fires of her concerns for her brother. After all, Priscilla Bunhead could have written a book entitled *Little Miss Busybody*.

Priscilla had suggested that I might want to make a friendly house call on her neighbor to check out the situation. Wouldn't you know it that Priscilla would go around the mulberry bush in order to try to get me involved! I held my tongue at her insinuations over someone about whom I didn't know the first thing. After all, I teach those classes in Advanced Holiness and I have to keep ever mindful about not casting judgments against others.

Well, I thought to myself, what could be the harm of checking up on one of our elderly parishioners? Besides, I always enjoyed the charming and handsome company of Jules. So, I filled my flask – er, my crucifix - with some heavenly spirits and I took off on foot for a contemplative stroll as I offered up a multitude of smoke signal-style prayers from my trusty Marlboros.

As I walked up the sidewalk to Jules' house, I happened to notice little Miss Busybody peering through her parted curtains. Her patch of bald scalp reflected the mid-afternoon sun like the burning broom of the wicked witch of the west. I gave her a curt smile and I mouthed to her, "I can see you!" She quickly disappeared from sight.

At the same time, on the other side of the house, I noticed Martha Mayhem out in her back yard. She was kicking at a pile of ashes and shouting, "Take that!" I wasn't sure what that was all about. I figured she just had another bone to pick with God; the poor misguided soul.

I must admit that I was a little taken back when Lula Mae, herself, answered Jules' front door. She was wearing a long, flowing, purple and scarlet caftan that had been cinched up at her bust line leaving nothing to the imagination. Her long, curly, and gleaming black hair was piled high on her head.

She was a bit surprised, herself, when she saw me standing on the doorstep in my own flowing black habit. She had been expecting Jules whom she'd sent out to Kentucky Fried Chicken. She was ravenous after their long journey.

Before I could open my mouth to speak, Lula Mae abruptly informed me that she was a Baptist and that she wasn't interested in hearing about any other religions. At least she had some manners since she ended her exclamation with a resounding "thank you!" Then, she slammed the door shut.

I wasn't about to be put off by her royal highness. I knocked again and, after a moment or two, she called out, "Baby," before she answered the door. I let her know that I was no baby, that I was here on a social call, and that I fully intended to wait for Jules to return.

Lula Mae answered, "Well, suits yo'self, sistah."

Then, she turned with a sweeping whoosh of her gown and she sashayed back into the living room. When she arrived at the sofa, she splayed her ample form on the sofa as if she was Cleopatra. It didn't take me long to tell that both Jules and I would have our work cut out for ourselves with this preening princess.

I closed the door behind me and I followed her into the room. Once there, I took my own seat and I quickly kissed my flip-top crucifix for a refreshing nip. Lord help us all!

That's when I heard Jules pull his car into the driveway. He didn't have a chance to make it into the house before he was verbally-assaulted by Martha Mayhem from two doors down the street. Not that I'm one to eavesdrop, but I could hear her surly words even with the front door closed. Apparently, so could Lula Mae.

As soon as Martha told Jules that she wasn't going to put up with him bringing home a floozy, Lula Mae flew off that sofa and right out the front door. She set those floorboards quaking beneath each of her purposeful steps. Lula Mae then barreled across the lawn of Prissy Bunhead and she launched herself at Martha Mayhem, knocking her right to the ground.

I wasn't sure whose bellows were louder after I heard Lula Mae demanding, "Who y'all callin' a ho?"

I refreshed myself as I braced myself with some of my heavenly spirits. I had my work cut out for me. As I crossed back over the threshold, I could see Poopsy Dinkledorf teetering out of his house on his rickety cane. In the meantime, Jules was valiantly trying to break up the fight, but Poopsy was enjoying the show. He enjoyed watching the two women flailing about. It brought back warm memories of the days when Daisy and Martha's mother, Maura, fought over him.

The show ended quickly once Martha Mayhem sunk her choppers into one of Lula Mae's billowing breasts. Lula Mae let out a bellow that could be heard all the way back at the convent. Lord, have mercy!

As I glanced to the west, I could see Prissy's bald pate shining like a spotlight. I could also see her look of utter disappointment when she saw that Martha had come out the victor. What could I do, but lend some sisterly support to the sobbing Lula Mae.

I helped Lula Mae to her feet, as Martha stomped off to the east, muttering to herself, "You haven't seen the last of me, you big, fat, black tart!"

Lula Mae stopped her blubbering as soon as she saw the king-sized containers from Kentucky Fried Chicken. There was nothing like fried chicken, biscuits, and gravy to soothe her soul. To Lula Mae's disappointment, I accepted Jules' dinner invitation. Yes indeed, God had sent me there today to provide some holy nourishment! Besides, I needed some nourishment of my own and I liked fried chicken myself.

Chapter 18

I returned to the convent just as Diddles Dinkledorf was pulling into our barn in his Chrysler Cordoba. Randy Cowboy met him at the gate. Randy had become rather fond of the old man and I could tell that he had been a good influence on Diddles, as well. Diddles had seemingly become more comfortable in his own skin.

I had started to notice that change after his wife, Babbetina, had passed on. Once Randy had come to work alongside him, Diddles had become more cheerful and more comfortable being around other men. I'd sometimes watch the two of them go on evening walks together. Whenever they'd return, Diddles would appear relaxed and smiling.

Of course, there were some people who casted judgments on their relationship, but I knew better. Even though Randy wore his gay colors freely, he was only interested in friendship with the older man. Randy had plenty of other cowboys and Indians with whom to play out on the range.

Every Friday and Saturday night, Randy would be off and running right after dinner was served. I knew what he was up to, but that was his business. I could tell that he was just a free spirit, though I wondered what a price his soul might pay for his no-strings encounters in the big city.

I'd have to remind myself that I was casting a judgment concerning something about which I had no knowledge or experience. After all, we're all in this life to learn our own lessons. Leave it to the busybodies like Priscilla Bunhead to mind other people's business.

I say, "How about tending to your own gardens? There are plenty of weeds growing in there while you're so concerned about what might be growing in other folk's gardens! Only the good Lord knows what lessons each of his children needs to learn."

Each of us has different lessons to learn and I knew it to be true that randy Randy hadn't had a particularly easy life. As I see it, Randy was really just looking for love; but, his sexploits never seemed to provide him with that possibility. He was always looking for the next high.

Yet, he never seemed to fulfill his quest. I guess that's just a part of what he'll need to discover for himself. After all, God loves each of us unconditionally, but we have to find that love within ourselves before we are truly ready to give and receive love.

When Diddles came home tonight, I noticed yet another new light in his eyes. I couldn't help but wonder what might have happened on his trip to Mississippi that had brought about this newest change in his attitude.

What I did observe was that he asked Randy to go for another stroll before Randy took off on his own adventures. When they came back, Diddles got himself spruced up and then he took off in his Chrysler Cordoba. If I hadn't known better, I would have sworn that he was off on a date. Well now! It would only be a matter of time before God would reveal the answer to that one.

In the meantime, it was time for me to get off to evening vespers. After all, it was the beginning of the

Advent season and we'd been gearing up for another joyful period of expectation for the coming of our Lord. What goes around, comes around; and, God knows how quickly the calendar flies before we all get to meet the Lord once again.

It seems like it was only yesterday that I was preparing for my first Advent season at the Have A Heart Convent! My own particular joy has always been preparing the little children for our annual Christmas Eve pageant. I will begin this year's rehearsals this coming week.

Sister Daniella Shakesalot put on a memorable performance during our evening vespers. The poor dear had recently come down with a raging case of the shaky-quakes. Yet, for her, it only served to enhance her own spiritual traditions. Let's just say that, when the Lord moves her, she moves us in the most mysterious ways.

Last night, we had barely filed into our pews when Sister Daniella was moved to move. That brave soul latched onto her walker and she teeter-tottered out into the aisle before the very first hymn. Sister Eileen McGillicutty accompanied her, because one never knows what Sister Daniella will do next when she's moved by the Holy Spirit.

That's when Lucy Lovely entered our chapel and began to proceed up the aisle. As Lucy Lovely was genuflecting before she entered a nearby pew, Sister Daniella reached out a long, quavering arm and she grabbed hold of Lucy Lovely's long hair.

As Sister Daniella nearly lost her balance, Sister Eileen grabbed onto her other arm. Lucy Lovely was struggling to free herself. That didn't stop Sister Daniella. She let go of Lucy Lovely's hair and she immediately latched onto her arm with a vise-like grip. That's when the real festivities were about to begin.

Our organist, Canty Playanote began to perform the introduction to our first hymn, *The Spirit Moves me in*

Mysterious Ways. With Sister Daniella in the middle, latched onto Lucy Lovely to her left and supported by Sister Eileen McGillicutty to her right, Sister Daniella was ready to roll.

She began to enter into a quaking wobble to the right which nearly pulled Lucy Lovely on top of her as Sister Eileen grabbed onto the pew to avoid falling right over. Not to worry, Sister Daniella began to wobble to the left, as she opened her mouth in a warbling sound of great joy.

Sister Daniella's entire body went into a spasm of rocking and rolling movements that left her two companions reeling alongside her while she began to sway at the same time. As she sang with increasing fervor, her movements became even more violent as she rocked Lucy Lovely and Sister Eileen with wild abandon. Even so, Sister Daniella's face reflected nothing other than sheer peaceful joy. It's just that her companions seemed possessed of a more frightening spirit.

If I hadn't known better, I could have sworn that the three of them were in a spinning car on a tilt-a-whirl amusement park ride. As the rocking and rolling reached a feverish pitch, Lucy Lovely's long mane was swirling around her head like a cowboy's lasso.

Mother Carmen had become noticeably perturbed and she approached the twirling trinity. As she reached toward Sister Daniella in order to bring her to a halt, Sister Daniella decided that it was time to get Mother into the spirit of the dance.

With her elbow now hooked onto Sister Eileen's, Sister Daniella reached out her free hand and she grabbed onto Mother Carmen's long veil. Before Mother Carmen knew what was happening next, she became a whirling dervish with that trio. That's when the other sisters decided that it was time to get into the spirit and to get into the act.

All of the nuns rocked themselves into the aisle as they

approached the swaying bodies and soaring spirits surrounding Sister Daniella. Before very long, the little chapel was filled with swirling habits as each of the other sisters latched onto the swaying masses. My Lord, I haven't seen such ecstasy since the days when the Mayhem sisters and Priscilla Bunhead were writhing to the strains of Elvis Presley! Let's just say that Elvis couldn't hold a torch to the pelvis of Sister Daniella. T-LIAM-G!

Chapter 19

*L*et me get back to the scene on Dinkledorf Drive. Now! Poopsy Dinkledorf always enjoyed antagonizing Martha Mayhem. He took such delight in stirring her up into one of her infamous tirades. Even though Prissy Bunhead had mistakenly thought that she had been secretly observing the fracas between Lula Mae and Martha, Poopsy Dinkledorf had noticed her.

In spite of all of the infirmities of old age that Poopsy had endured, his vision was still as keen as a hawk. Poopsy had noticed that Prissy was visibly disappointed that Martha had been the victor. He decided he'd see if he could stir things up a bit and get another female wrestling match going on the block.

What Poopsy didn't know was that Priscilla was already set to duel with Martha once again. Having lost her precious bun to mean Martha was yet another reminder of that long ago night when Prissy was exposed and humiliated in her swimming pool. Every time Priscilla looked in the mirror, her shining scalp reminded her of both of her public exposures that had been orchestrated by Martha. She decided it was time to teach her a lesson; so, Prissy was too busy to answer the door when Poopsy came a-calling. Poor Poopsy!

Priscilla knew that the Mayhem family was holding a family reunion two weeks before Christmas. She decided that she was going to set Martha up for a fall. Knowing that Martha was estranged from her family, Priscilla typed a note to Martha that she hoped would entice Martha to come to the reunion. Priscilla's plan was to get Martha to the reunion where she would then be humiliated herself.

Priscilla felt wonderfully wicked as she drafted her baiting note. She wrote a note of apology, asking for Martha's forgiveness, as if it was coming from Martha's sisters, Mildred and Myrtle. She milked it for all it was worth.

In the forged note, the sisters both told Martha how wrong they had been not to make her godmother of their children. After all, Martha had no children of her own. The note conceded that she would have been better able to fulfill that role.

Priscilla, as Mildred, elaborated by saying that her precious daughter, Dimples, had always regarded Martha as her favorite aunt. "Mildred" expressed her remorse for having created a distance between them. Priscilla concluded the note by asking Martha to forgive and forget by attending the reunion as the honored elder sister and aunt. Then, Priscilla completed her forgery by signing the note with the sisters' signatures.

As luck would have it, Martha took the bait. She even went out and bought herself a party dress. It was the first dress she had bought for herself in nearly fifty years. Then, she went to the local beauty parlor and she had her hair done up for the occasion. Martha had decided to let bygones be bygones. She was going to give her family another chance. After all, she didn't have any real friends and she was tired of being lonely.

Priscilla wanted to be on hand for the big event. She'd always wielded some influence over the Mayhem girls, with Martha being the only exception. Mildred Mayflower and Myrtle Merriweather had served as strong examples within her BUN Organization. Oh, how Priscilla just loved her clever acronym for "Bunheads Unite Now!"

Well! Priscilla demurely approached her fellow bunheads, the Mayhem girls. Then, she asked them if she could serve as hostess at their family reunion.

When the reunion day had finally arrived, Priscilla was in all of her glory. She'd gone out and bought herself a new fake bun which she had somehow managed to attach to the wisps of hair that had started to sprout on her bald pate. Priscilla was going to have the last laugh when the supposed guest of honor arrived. After all, Martha hadn't even received a legitimate invitation. She'd already made it clear to the rest of the family that there wasn't a snowball's chance in hell that she'd attend the reunion.

Martha showed up an hour after the reunion had begun. Priscilla had purposefully given her the wrong time. Everyone else was already licking their chops on the main course of prime rib au jus when Martha arrived. At first, she seemed confused. Well, truth be told, so were the other family members. Martha stormed up to her sister, Mildred and she asked Mildred how she had dared to serve dinner before the guest of honor had arrived. Mildred was baffled and she asked who this guest of honor was.

That's when Martha shouted, "It's me!"

That's also when Priscilla Bunhead made her grand entrance. With a wicked smile upon her face, Priscilla marched defiantly up toward the ensuing mayhem. Then, Priscilla whispered to Martha, "How does it feel to be caught naked without even a bun to keep you warm?"

All of a sudden, the lights finally went on for Martha. True to form, she grabbed the carving knife off the roast beef serving platter; and then, in one swift movement, she severed Priscilla's fake bun. Finally, with bun in hand, she ran to the roaring fireplace and she threw Prissy's bun into the oven. Once again, the woman named Bunhead looked more like the pinhead that she was.

It's just too bad for Poopsy Dinkledorf that he didn't get to witness the ensuing brouhaha. When Priscilla and Martha went into the ring, it made Martha's duel with Lula Mae look like child's play. The only similarity to child's play in this instance was that the two sixty-five year-olds had behaved like a couple of grade-school girls.

Word travels fast in the small town of Bucksnort and Poopsy soon caught wind of the reunion bash. He chuckled to himself as he saw Martha Mayhem return home with her party dress ripped right down to her midriff. Poopsy was amazed to see that Martha was so well-endowed. He just loved a full-figured gal. Martha had always disguised whatever shapeliness she had left by wearing shapeless shifts and over-sized men's clothing.

Poopsy teetered out of his house on his rickety cane to get a closer look at her goods. He'd never lost interest in women or sexual matters, though he was long past his hey day and he wasn't interested in any women over seventy. Most of the women he found attractive were young enough to be his daughters or granddaughters; and, to them, he was just too old. Consequently, he had gained a reputation for himself as being a dirty old man.

Poopsy tempted fate when he called out to Martha, "I hear you got in a few licks with Prissy Bunhead. Looks to me like she got the better of you!"

That was all Martha needed to hear at that point. She was still fuming at the dirty trick that Priscilla had played on her and she had plenty of venom left. She turned in Poopsy's direction and she snorted, "Don't start messing with me, old man! I'll come right over, knock out your cane, and put you right on the ground."

Poopsy chuckled as he said, "You're getting me excited, Martha." Then, he winked and he leered as he said, "I sure like the look of your fancy party dress. How'd you like to take a little moonlight stroll with me?"

Martha retorted, "Don't flatter yourself, you old geezer! If you look over yonder, you'll see the stairway to heaven is right there waiting for you."

Poopsy ignored her comment and he didn't miss a beat when he asked, "How about you and me building a bonfire out back to warm ourselves by?"

Martha let out a harrumph and she stormed into her house, but Poopsy was in no hurry to call it an evening. He was in the mood for some mischief. That's when he heard some loud female moaning coming from the direction of Jules Jesslike Pappas' house. Poopsy started shuffling in the direction of the sounds.

It took him quite awhile, but he was determined. He was especially determined as the intensity of that moaning increased. Poopsy was getting excited. He drew closer to Jules' home and he approached the dimly-lit bedroom window. He thought he'd just have a little looksy for himself, but Poopsy wasn't as tall as he used to be. His eyes were barely level with the window sill. What was he to do? He was mighty curious to see what all of the commotion was about. That's when he spotted a metal bucket next to the edge of the house.

He hobbled over to the bucket, grabbed it with his spare hand, and he returned with it to the bedroom window. The moaning was getting louder all the time. Poopsy didn't have a minute to spare. He placed that bucket upside-down beneath the window and he prepared to mount it.

Poor Poopsy! He wasn't as sure-footed as he used to be. As he climbed onto that bucket, he lost his balance and he crashed his head into the window. He just got himself one glimpse of Lula Mae's wriggling body before she let out a scream. He grabbed that windowsill and held onto it, never taking his eyes off Lula Mae's voluptuous form as she rose off that bed in a hurry. That's when Poopsy decided he'd better get a move on.

He lowered himself off the bucket and he lost his footing for a second time, falling onto the hard, cold ground. Before he could even think about getting upright again, Poopsy had company and the company was not amused!

As Poopsy got onto his knees on all fours, Lula Mae grabbed Poopsy's cane and she gave him a whack right on his bony butt. There was a time when he might have enjoyed that kind of whack, but he didn't have any padding left with which to absorb the shock wave. It hurt, but it was worth it.

As he fell back onto the ground, he got another good look at Lula Mae while he gazed up into her billowing dressing gown. He thought to himself that maybe Martha was right. Perhaps it was time for him to take a walk up that stairway to heaven. "Nope," was his second thought. He was still having too much fun in the "right here and now."

Chapter 20

"T-LIAM-G, my dears! This is Sister Mary Olga Fortitude coming to you. Now! The Advent season is upon us, my children, and it's a good time for all of you students of Advanced Holiness to meditate upon the true meaning of Christmas. Isn't it a pity that so many people become wrapped up in the frenzy of the material world? So many of us get so busy buying things that people don't really need. Then, we only end up feeding that empty aching place of want."

"Yes, my dears, I imagine that God looks down from heaven with sadness upon all of His children who are scurrying around trying to buy those perfect presents. Guess what? He's already given us the perfect present. The baby Jesus represents the light and hope for this dark and lonely world. All we have to do is to remember to ask and we shall receive this great gift – the love and the peace of Christ."

"Now! You've heard me tell some tales of where that lonely, aching place of want can take people. They seem to think that there's something they can grab from this physical world that will ease the pain of loneliness - something that will fill up that seeming aching hole of separation that only God can fill."

"They take everything so seriously as they get caught up with all of their human emotions, acting them out in the most childish ways. Really! If everyone could just take a time-out and look down upon themselves, I think they'd really get an eye-opener!"

"Still, we must practice patience and tolerance. If only we could look at all the ways that we act out our emotions and just have a sense of humor, perhaps we could get back on track. That's why I've been telling you human stories that will hopefully hit you right in your funny bone. Maybe you can even see yourselves when you reflect upon your own behaviors and human weaknesses."

"Just be careful not to judge some of my favorite parishioners. Even though you may not be able to relate to some of their own life challenges, I ask you to consider how you may create the difficulties as well as the joys within your own lives. Yes, Christmas is a time for reflection as well as a time for great joy. Jesus has come again!"

"Oh, oh! Be careful, my children. Even though many of us are blessed to have received the message of hope that Jesus brings to us, let us remember that many people have different faith traditions. Let us not impose our beliefs upon others who may have different beliefs."

"I say, whatever floats your boat! As long as one practices a faith that leads them to a better place, who are we to judge? After all, God made us all different for a reason. We must learn to love and respect those who are different than ourselves. When we lose sight of this, we are going to a place of fear and judgment rather than one of faith and love."

Now! You may have been wondering where Diddles Dinkledorf set off to on that evening he returned to the Have A Heart Convent. Well, my dears, he had love in his heart and he had made a decision that he wanted to go for his joy. He was tired of living a lie that came from a place of fear. He had found faith in himself. He decided it was high time to be true to himself.

You may recall that Diddles had gotten his own eye-opener when he had made his trip to Mississippi. After all of those years of hiding from his true feelings, he had realized that he was actually in love with Mark Mayhem. He wasn't getting any younger and he had decided right then and there that it was time to let Mark know how he really felt.

Well, Diddles got himself all spruced up on that night of his return and he took off to pay a call on Mark. First, he made a visit to the confessional and Father Cowberries. Mind you, I was just wrapping up a confession of my own and I was no longer feeling any pain. It always helps to unburden oneself; and, I must admit, the refreshment of the confessional always has a double benefit for me.

In spite of my state of relaxation, I noticed that there was something different about Diddles that evening. I figured that Randy Cowboy would fill me in on the details later.

Anyhow, Diddles spoke to Father Cowberries about his lifelong affair with Mark Mayhem as he poured out his heart about his new understanding of his love for him. Father Cowberries wasn't exactly sure what to say. He knew what the Pope would have to say, but Father Cowberries had his own cross to bear on the subject.

When he had been in the seminary, he had found himself conflicted over feelings that he had had for a fellow seminarian. He had always been taught that it was a sin for a man to have sex with another man; but, Lord, had he ever been tempted! The thing is, he had never been able to let go of his yearning for this fellow and it had continued to haunt him for the rest of his life.

Now, here was Father Cowberries listening to another soul pour himself out over his yearning for another man. What was he to say? Father Cowberries was stumped. That's when he turned to the Holy Spirit for guidance and when he remembered the larger lesson of love taught by Jesus.

Consequently, Father let go of the programming of man and he spoke from his heart. He told Diddles that he had nothing of which to be guilty or ashamed. Whenever love is present and one is true to oneself, how could there be anything wrong? After Father had spoken, both he and Diddles each felt as if they had been relieved of a tremendous burden.

Afterwards, Diddles drove off into the night in his Chrysler Cordoba with the hope that Mark would open his heart to him. Unfortunately for Diddles, Mark was not on the same page as he was. He met Mark at Burger Heaven. That's when Diddles poured his heart out once more.

Mark stared back at Diddles with incomprehension. He reminded Diddles that he was married and that he was straight. He told Diddles that what the two of them did together was only about a type of sex that he couldn't get from his wife. That's when Mark told Diddles that he couldn't see him anymore. Diddles was beside himself with his grief.

He got back into his Chrysler Cordoba and he drove off into the night, not knowing where he would go. The only place he could think of was to go back to the confessional with Father Cowberries. He needed something – anything - to lift his spirits from his dark place of despair.

Chapter 21

The Advent season moved along quickly and, once again, it was time for the annual children's Christmas Eve pageant. Most of the members of our parish showed up for the event; that is, everyone except Martha Mayhem. I was surprised to see that Marjorine Mayhem was alone. I wondered where Mark was. All of his grandchildren had roles in our play. Diddles Dinkledorf was present along with the rest of the Dinkledorf clan to watch his grandson, Fartley, in his debut as the baby Jesus.

I couldn't help but notice that Diddles didn't seem to be himself. He looked lost and he appeared to be in another place. I decided right then and there that I would definitely have to have a talk with Randy Cowboy right after Christmas.

Oh yes, it was going to be a festive night! Amanda Ann Adult was busy in the kitchen preparing a delicious banquet to be enjoyed by the crowd. I must confess that I kept slipping into the kitchen to see if I could be of any help. I knew that Amanda Ann would be busy sampling her holiday egg nog as she prepared the food. I certainly thought that she could use a second opinion on the nog. Apparently, so did Father Cowberries!

My goodness, the three of us were so busy sampling the

egg nog that I nearly lost track of the time! I needed to run the children through a last minute rehearsal before the banquet would begin. The grand event of the evening would be the children's performance, followed by caroling by all. Then, it would be time for Father Cowberries to lead the parish in a midnight Christmas Eve mass.

Little Fartley Dinkledorf was in all of his glory since he had the leading role in our pageant. I reminded him that he was representing our perfect Lord Jesus and that I expected him to behave as the perfect baby he was honored to portray. Fartley's little sister, Dewdrop Dinkledorf, was going to be one of the sheep and two of Mark and Marjorine Mayhem's grandsons were to play the ox and the ass.

Myrtle Merriweather's granddaughter, Ivy, had another leading role as Mary. I took a chance on the oldest Mayhem grandson, Muchmore Mayhem, having given him the role of Joseph. Of course, there were other children to play the rest of the roles, though I had the girls play the roles of the shepherd and the wise men. The remaining boys in my class became the camels.

I must confess that I was almost as excited as the children and their families. That gave me a good excuse to run into the kitchen every so often to have another glass of Amanda Ann's egg nog to calm my nerves. I was a little annoyed that Father Cowberries had just stationed himself by the punch bowl. Good Lord, Father, save some egg nog for the rest of us!

Well now! Every one had eaten and it was time for the show to begin. A reverent hush fell over the audience as the stage curtain lifted to show Mary and Joseph standing outside the door of the inn. Alas, there was no room in the inn and the lights dimmed as our little actors reassembled in the manger.

I was in a near swoon after my many trips to the punch

bowl. I had also nearly forgotten to wrap our baby Jesus in swaddling clothes and to lay him in the manger. At least, Fartley had prepared by stripping down to his underwear. Alas, he hadn't helped matters much since he had been shocking all of the little girls. He'd been backing up to one of the Christmas candles where he'd been igniting one blaze after another by passing gas through the flame.

Muchmore Mayhem had followed his example, though he couldn't hold a candle to Fartley's talents. I severely reprimanded them and I threatened to take the role of baby Jesus away from Fartley. He promised me he would behave. What else could I do except to believe him?

All was in readiness now for our divine drama. Before the stage lights came up, all of the little children sang *Away in the Manger*. Oh, it was going to be a lovely pageant! Another hush fell over the audience as the lights came up on our manger scene. Little Ivy looked adoringly as she hummed the same carol to her little baby Jesus.

Just as I thought that everything was going to be perfect, a loud ripping sound erupted from the cradle. I couldn't contain myself. I caught myself in mid-syllable when I exclaimed, "Fart!" That's when I gave Fartley a glare that would sink a battleship.

He returned my look with a beatific smile just before he erupted in laughter and proclaimed, "It was the ass!"

That's when Joseph and all of the camels started laughing uncontrollably. Suddenly, I noticed Mother Carmen Burana rise from her seat and start striding toward the stage. Now I knew there was going to be some really hot wind. The audience started shifting nervously in their seats.

I could tell Mother was struggling to maintain her composure as she mounted the stage and hissed at me, "Sister Mary OLGA Fortitude! You seem to have the wrong baby for Jesus!"

Then, she turned to the audience and she announced, "The pageant is over!" That's when she called out for Father Cowberries to come and lead the audience in Christmas carols.

What Mother Carmen Burana didn't know was that Father Cowberries and Amanda Ann Adult were busy finishing up the egg nog in the kitchen while Amanda Ann was struggling to finish the icing on her Noel log cake. Amanda Ann was slightly beside herself because she couldn't seem to get her cake decorator to work properly. Father Cowberries offered to assist her in the matter, but Amanda Ann was getting pretty testy.

Neither of them were balancing all too well on their feet. When Father Cowberries reached for the cake decorator, Amanda Ann pushed him away with a little too much vigor. That's all it took to tip the tipsy Father headlong into the holiday cake.

Meanwhile, Mother Carmen was getting pretty testy herself. I could almost see the steam coming out from under her stiff collar. Once again, Mother Carmen summoned the parish priest, but this time she bellowed out his name. Well, what was the padre to do? He pulled his head out of the cake and he stumbled out from the kitchen looking like the Pillsbury Dough Boy.

He licked his frosting-covered mouth and then he started to sing *The First Nowell.* Meanwhile, the rest of the audience was treated to the background vocals of Amanda Ann Adult who was cursing a blue streak.

Little Dewdrop Dinkledorf saved the day when she stepped forward in her sheep's costume and started quietly singing *Silent Night.* Father Cowberries was momentarily confused, but the audience took their cue from little Dewdrop and they started singing right along with her.

Wouldn't you know it, but Amanda Ann Adult decided she was going to take center stage. She came barreling out of the kitchen with her Yule log that looked as if it had been attacked by a hungry beaver.

She pushed it front and center as she swayed and slurred, "Dessert is now served even though Father Cowberries couldn't wait for his piece!"

With all of the commotion, I decided to take my opportunity to make my getaway. I decided the kitchen was probably the safest place in which to escape. Thank goodness, Amanda Ann and Father Cowberries hadn't finished all of the egg nog! I was beginning to feel especially thirsty.

I spotted an empty pitcher and I filled it from the punch bowl. Then, I headed for the sanctuary of cubicle number four. God knows I needed some strength in order to get through the rest of the evening!

One thing was certain. There would be hell to pay come Christmas Day. I only hoped that Mother Carmen would remember the meaning of Christmas and let me off the hook for my part in the pageant fiasco.

Chapter 22

*C*hristmas Day arrived and I was paying a price. My head felt as if it would explode. I didn't feel any better when I was summoned to Mother Carmen's chambers before breakfast. I had been expecting the worst and I had already put on my knee pads. Mother had another surprise in store for me, but I can't say that it made me feel any better than the thought of spending another week in solitary contemplation on my knees.

"Sister Mary Olga Fortitude," she began. "Last night's demonstration during our Christmas pageant has made it clear to me that we have some real behavioral problems among some of your boys."

She went on to say, "I've contacted Marjorine Mayhem and Blinky Dinkledorf to discuss a plan." Blinky was married to Dinky Dinkledorf and they were the parents of Fartley.

I quickly kissed my crucifix for a little strength before Mother Carmen went on to say, "They are in complete agreement that the Mayhem boys and little Fartley need to learn a lesson in reverence. What I have proposed is that these boys shall have to forgo their Christmas vacation and spend the week with you teaching them lessons in Remedial Holiness. After all, I hold you directly responsible for the state of their spirituality as well as for that ungodly behavior we all had to witness last night. I only hope that I can be assured of your cooperation and success with this venture. The boys will report to you first thing in the morning."

"By the way," she added. "I've asked Father Cowberries to be available to assist you. You may go now, Sister!"

"Good Lord!" I thought. "This shall be another cross for me to bear." Of course, the one thing I knew to be true was that the Lord never gives any of us any more than we can handle. I would just have to look for the silver lining in this seemingly dark cloud.

Well! I immediately went in search of Father Cowberries after I left Mother's office. I was certain that both of us would need some fortification in order to come up with a plan.

I found Father Cowberries in the chapel, getting ready for his Christmas mass. He looked rather forlorn not to mention a little green around the gills. I imagined I probably looked the same to him. He spoke to me with a pained expression, "A blessed Merry Christmas to you, Sister."

"The same to you, Father," I said.

He went on to say, "Whatever are we going to do Sister? It's not that I believe that those boys are beyond redemption, but we certainly will have a handful!"

I suggested that we pray together in his confessional. Let me add that our prayers were both refreshing and inspirational!

The two of us decided we needed to get away from under the scrutiny of Mother Carmen; so, we decided to go on a retreat with the boys. I quickly made arrangements with Amanda Ann Adult to handle the catering for our affair. Then, I put in a call to the Mayhems and the Dinkledorfs. We would leave first thing in the morning.

I must say that we were all in excellent spirits when we departed from the convent on the following day. We loaded the boys in the back of the academy's station wagon as we set off on our adventure at the parish's wilderness retreat which was located on a nearby lake.

The boys were all excited, but I reminded them that this was not a vacation. We were headed to the wilds to learn and perform the work of God. That sobered them up for awhile. Unfortunately, Father and I had to remain sober if we were going to serve as good caregivers to the boys. Of course, that didn't preclude a few nips after lights out!

By the time we reached our retreat house, the boys were still in high spirits. Unfortunately, Father Cowberries and I were both already exhausted. After all, the past two days had taken a toll on us. We showed the boys to the dormitory and we made the bed assignments. Our first class in Remedial Holiness was scheduled to begin right after lunchtime.

Wouldn't you know it, little Fartley Dinkledorf was nowhere to be found when class was scheduled to begin! The Mayhem boys didn't seem particularly perturbed, but I was still fuming over his untimely fumes during the Christmas pageant. I asked Father Cowberries to go in search of Fartley so that I could at least start Remedial Holiness with those Mayhem monsters... er, those precious little boys!

After an hour of drilling the Mayhems on the dos and don'ts of holiness, Father Cowberries burst into the classroom in tears. He exclaimed, "I can't find Fartley anywhere!"

Good Lord, wouldn't you know it? That child would do anything to get me into an unholy snit! Well! Our class had already been disrupted; so, I decided we would all go in search of our missing angel-in-training. We divided up into two search parties. Muchmore Mayhem accompanied

Father Cowberries and I had the two younger Mayhems in tow.

I couldn't understand why it would be so difficult to find the lad. After all, there were little footprints in the snow. It didn't even appear as if Father Cowberries had discovered the trail.

The Mayhem boys and I started following the footprints which meandered through the woods for some good distance. Close to the end of those footprints, they suddenly veered around a large evergreen tree. Shortly thereafter, those little footprints came to an end right near a set of larger footprints that nearly crossed their path.

I couldn't help but think of the poem *Footprints* when we'd reached the end of the trail. Where could that boy have disappeared to? I thought he was far from ready to receive his wings and to be lifted up by God.

Then, it dawned on me what had happened. Fartley must have hidden behind that evergreen tree when he'd heard Father Cowberries approach during his initial search for the lad. Once the coast was clear, he'd jumped into Father Cowberries' footprints and he had followed them back to the retreat house. He must have hidden somewhere nearby while the rest of us had started off on our search. I sure couldn't wait until the end of the day when Father Cowberries and I could have some refreshments!

We never got that chance. Fartley had set us up! That little devil had had the nerve to call Mother Carmen back at the Have A Heart Convent. He'd told her that he'd been left all alone at the retreat house and that he was hungry. The result of that call was that our retreat was canceled by Mother.

My explanation about how Fartley had engineered his sneaky solitude was to have been of no avail. Mother Carmen said that it was obvious that I didn't have control of the boys and that she, herself, would teach those classes in Remedial Holiness back at the Academy. She had another mission in mind for me.

It's a good thing that I had found my kneepads. Now, here I am once again. I am sequestered in my cell to contemplate my transgressions. I didn't even have a chance to sneak in a bottle of Old Granddad with me. Mother Carmen had quickly dispatched me into my cell immediately upon my return. Lord have mercy! I shall be seeing in the New Year in solitude in my solitary confinement.

Chapter 23

T-LIAM-G, my dears! This is Sister Mary Olga Fortitude coming to you. Now! I'm happy to report that Mother Carmen had mercy on me and sprang me from my cell in time for the New Year's Eve vespers. Well! I might not have had much success with my class in Remedial Holiness; but, thank God, I still had my devoted students of Advanced Holiness!

As I've told you before, one of my most diligent students has been Lucy Lovely. Even so, I've continued to have concerns for her susceptibility to the ways of the world since she occasionally reverts to her bunhead ways. She'd better be careful when Martha Mayhem's around or she might just get her bun lopped off. If that was to be the case, she might as well put on a wimple and habit. She'd certainly make a marvelous nun!

I had the biggest surprise in my class the other evening. Who do you think showed up? It was none other than the oldest and most delinquent member of our parish, Poopsy Dinkledorf. I almost suggested to him that he was in the wrong class and that, perhaps, he was looking for the class in Remedial Holiness. Fortunately, I behaved appropriately. I held my tongue.

I shouldn't have been surprised when he took a seat

right next to Lucy Lovely. I couldn't really blame him for being distracted by her beauty. It's just that his attentiveness to her would eventually become a problem. I, myself, soon became distracted by the old man's leering looks toward my favorite student. As it turned out, I didn't have to wait long before Lucy Lovely dealt with the situation in her own way.

She swung her head with that mane of hair following in a sweep as she screamed at Poopsy, "Stop staring at me, old man!"

That didn't ruffle Poopsy's feathers at all. In fact, he rather seemed to enjoy Lucy Lovely's outburst. In fact, he moved his chair an inch or two closer to her as he "tee-hee-heed" to himself. He reached out and touched Lucy Lovely's silken hair.

"Lord have mercy!" I thought. "Perhaps I would have to take remedial action."

Not to worry, Lucy Lovely simply gave him a look that would sink a battleship as she gathered up her books and her handbag. Then, she paraded to the other side of the room.

As she did so, Poopsy got out of his chair and he began to teeter-totter after her. That's when Lucy Lovely turned and said, "Don't even think about that, old man!"

With that said, she seated herself demurely. Then, she reached into her handbag, got out a bun clip, and she coiled her long hair into a tight little bun.

Well! I decided it was time to change my lesson plan for the evening. Tonight's topic would be "respect." Wouldn't you know it, at that very minute, Martha Mayhem walked into the room. Now, I really knew that God had provided me with the right topic!

Martha took the only seat that was left right behind Lucy Lovely. Then she cast a look of disgust at Lucy Lovely's bunhead. Meanwhile, on the other side of the room, Poopsy was still in high spirits. He looked in Martha's direction and he winked at her. She responded with an audible snort and a glare. Lord knows, I had a challenge on my hands! I reverently kissed my crucifix for a long and refreshing moment.

"Now class!" I began. "Let us all take a moment to meditate on the meaning of loving one another."

Poopsy let go with another one of his "tee-hee-hees."

"Poopsy Dinkledorf," I said. "Perhaps you could tell us exactly what you find so amusing. It might do all of us good to have a laugh."

Poopsy smiled with a twinkle in his eye as he said, "I know at least two ladies in this room who I'd like to do a little loving with."

"Good Lord, Poopsy Dinkledorf! That's a good example of something that has little to do with respect."

It certainly was high time for me to get a better answer for the meaning of loving one another. I posed my question to the class. Even though she hadn't raised her hand, I knew that I'd get a good answer from Lucy Lovely so I called upon her to answer the question.

She blushed, but then she answered the question in a voice as sweet and clear as a pealing church bell, "To truly love another person, you have to see them through new eyes in each passing moment. That way you are giving them the respect of truly seeing them for who they are instead of who you want them to be."

That's when I gave her a resounding, "Yes! I couldn't have put it any better myself, my dear!"

Somewhere else in the room, I heard someone muttering in a disagreeable tone. I zeroed in on the culprit. It was none other than Martha Mayhem. She obviously took issue with Lucy Lovely's perfect answer to my question. She was also staring with disgust at Lucy's bunhead and I guess that I should have expected that there might be trouble.

Suddenly Martha Mayhem reached forward and she grabbed Lucy Lovely's bun clip while she muttered, "There is nothing perfectly lovely about a bunhead!"

Lucy whirled around in her seat with such a fury that her tightly coiled hair spun around her head like a lasso and it momentarily resembled a cobra snake. Something not so lovely was about to happen.

With all of the venom of a striking snake, Lucy Lovely's voice became as tight and shrill as a violin string as she shrieked at Martha Mayhem, "You touched my hair, you wicked old witch! Give me back my bun clip right now!"

Martha Mayhem puffed out her chest and she rose out of her seat. Double trouble was on the way. I could just hear Martha's tone rising like a jet that was revving up its engine for a take off.

She snarled, "I'm getting pretty sick and tired of you perfect and prissy princesses parading around this town with your ugly bunheads. The next time I catch you with a bun, you may end up a bun short, just like Prissy Bunhead! How'd you like that, princess?"

Lucy Lovely wasn't about to back down and I must confess that I was proud of her. Forgive me Lord, but I always enjoy seeing someone take down Martha Mayhem a peg or two. Lucy Lovely rose out of her chair and she put her hands on her hips. Being as statuesque as a model, she towered over Martha's puffed-out, short and stout form which resembled that of a bullfrog. On the other side of the room, I could hear Poopsy Dinkledorf delightedly giggling in a gaggle of "tee-hee-hees" as Lucy opened her mouth to speak.

This time, she spoke slowly and clearly as she said, "In this moment, I see you as nothing more than a frightened little child, old woman. You can't intimidate me; so, you might as well just give it up. In the spirit of Advanced Holiness, I shall try to look on you with loving eyes; and, I forgive you. Just don't try to mess with me again!"

Oh Lord, I couldn't help myself but I led the entire class in a round of applause. I was exuberant as I said, "Touche', Lucy Lovely! You have just given us all a lesson in self-respect along with the holy and loving message of forgiveness. You may be excused in order to fix your lovely hair. As for you, Martha Mayhem and Poopsy Dinkledorf, you will not be allowed in this class until you both complete another course in Remedial Holiness. Class dismissed!"

Chapter 24

*G*ood Lord! I almost forgot about my concern for Diddles Dinkledorf. Now! Having his disruptive father in my class was a blessing in disguise since it served as a reminder of my previous intentions. I rushed out of the classroom and I made a beeline to Randy Cowboy's quarters.

I found Randy having one of his little chats on the Internet. Randy quickly turned off his computer monitor, but I caught a glimpse of the party to whom he was chatting. He had just emailed Randy a picture of himself that left nothing to the imagination. Randy thought I didn't notice; but, after teaching little children for so many decades, there aren't too many tricks that escape my attention.

I must say, it looked to me as if Randy was planning on a little trick or treat even though Halloween was nearly a year away! Still, I had to remember that Randy wasn't a little child; and, besides, who was I to judge? Whatever goes on between two consenting adults is only between them and God. Randy's a good soul and it certainly wasn't any of my business!

I was grateful that Randy offered me a tumbler of Jack Daniel's. I was rather parched, not to mention a little stressed-out following the outbursts in my classroom. I started chain-smoking my Marlboros in contemplation of what I wanted to discuss with Randy. The poor dear was a bit distracted, but I didn't let that distract me from my mission. I wanted to find out what was troubling Diddles.

Randy filled me in on the sad tale of Diddles' profession of love to Mark Mayhem, followed by his rejection. Oh, the human condition can be filled with such misery! It's so unnecessary if people would only stop to think of the hurt they can cause one another by careless inconsideration of others' feelings.

I must confess that I initially passed a judgment against Mark. I thought to myself, "He's nothing but a sexaholic of the worst kind." Then, I thought of dear Randy who was a self-professed sex maniac who would never purposefully hurt anyone else. I decided that my judgment of Mark Mayhem was too kind. He was nothing but a deceitful user of people, not to mention one of being an unfaithful husband to Marjorine. Oh Lord, there I go with my judgments again! Father, forgive me.

I must say that Randy brought me up a bit short when he advised me I really shouldn't be discussing other peoples' concerns behind their backs. He suggested that I go directly to the source if I was truly concerned. Hmm! What wisdom from someone who has never taken my course in Advanced Holiness!

I must admit that I was in no hurry to leave Randy's quarters. I hadn't had my fill of Jack Daniel's and my cigarettes were oh, so delicious. Never mind! I could tell that Randy was anxious to get back to his good buddy, so I bid him goodnight.

Now! The very next morning, I paid a visit upon Diddles at his workshop. I decided it was finally time for me to make my amends to him for having blackmailed him concerning his relationship with Mark for so many years. Besides, now that Randy Cowboy was "homo" on the range, if you'll pardon my poor pun, I had another source for my own vices. Just kidding!

Diddles looked so glum when I knocked on his shop door. My heart went out to him. I decided not to beat around the bush; so, I told him I was aware of his personal situation and I offered to be of service if he needed to talk it out.

Diddles broke down and cried, "Oh, Sister Mary Olga! I'm so sad."

He proceeded to pour his heart out to me and my own heart melted even more because he was placing his trust in me. I felt very humble. I asked him if he would like for me to try to talk with that scoundrel, Mark Mayhem. Diddles suddenly became quite anxious and said he wasn't sure if that was a very good idea. That's when a light bulb lit up for me.

I suggested he talk with Father Cowberries about his situation. Perhaps Father could have a friendly chat with Mark Mayhem to help him see the errors of his ways. Diddles was pretty nervous about that suggestion.

Diddles thought it over. Then, he told me that he thought it might be better, after all, if I approached Mark. He thought it might be less threatening than a visit from the parish priest. He didn't want to rock the boat any more than necessary. After all, Marjorine had been after Mark to take my class in Advanced Holiness for years; so, she wouldn't have any suspicions about me meeting with him.

I had one final piece of business to settle with Diddles before I left. I confessed that I was wrong to have blackmailed him for so many years and that it had weighed heavily on my soul. I asked for his forgiveness and he answered me with a warm smile. T-LIAM-G!

Chapter 25

T-LIAM-G, my dears! This is Sister Mary Olga Fortitude coming to you. Now! I'm going to tell you a strange story if you'll promise to keep my secret. You see, my secret involves someone else's secret that was shared with me. I must confess that I take liberties with other people's business when I tell you my stories; however, let's just remember that it's for the sake of Advanced Holiness. So, I trust that the Lord won't mind!

Now! We started off the New Year in a most joyful fashion at the convent. I've told you about our rather dire need for new nuns. Well, the Lord is good and He has blessed us with a new bride of Christ. She arrived on New Year's Day.

Her name is Sister Samantha Monet and she is an exquisite creature, if I must say so myself. Mind you, beauty is as beauty does; but, I was so taken with her delicate features that I almost began to question my own sexuality.

She is a diminutive and young Italian goddess with a perfect complexion. Her rosy cheeks are like apples, her lips are shaped like a heart, and she has the cutest little dimple on her chin. Her smile lights up her soulful hazel eyes with an inviting dance to join her in the festival of life. Yet, it is her vivacious personality that I believe will win over new converts to Jesus.

Sister Samantha is a nurse who will be serving our academy as well as our older sisters who require tender loving care in their declining years. She has such a zest for life. She will undoubtedly be a wonderful role model for young women in our parish who might be contemplating a holy vocation. Yes, the Lord has sent us an angel who has been an answer to our prayers.

Now! I'm sure you're all curious about her secret. Let's not forget that curiosity killed the cat; and, Sister Samantha wouldn't be too happy about that. She also happens to be an ardent pet lover and she has plans to open an animal shelter for stray animals in our parish. Oh yes, things are definitely looking up at the Have A Heart convent!

Speaking of looking up, that brings me to the subject of Sister Samantha's secret. Lord, have mercy! Well now! I was extremely thirsty following my most recent week of penance on my knees in my humble little cell; so, I'd made a hasty visit to Randy Cowboy who was generous enough to give me a half gallon of Jack Daniel's.

I threw caution to the wind and I ducked into cubicle number four where I began to have a few nips. Oh, I must confess the truth. I tied one on! By the time I'd passed out, I'd managed to refresh myself with almost half of that big bottle. Oh my!

Sometime during the night, I must have slipped off the toilet and landed on the floor. I didn't wake up until the following morning; and, I must say, I had quite a headache! I also realized that I had partially slid under cubicle number three; and, I couldn't get up.

Well, wouldn't you know it, the restroom door burst open and I immediately thought that the gig was up. With my luck, I thought that it might be Mother Carmen and that I'd be sent back to my cell for another week of solitary confinement.

Fortunately, God spared me that ordeal and He had sent me an angel. It was Sister Samantha. Of course, I didn't find that out immediately. Let's just say that we both had a big surprise in store!

Well! There I was, with my head under cubicle number three, when I heard Sister Samantha singing *Amazing Grace* as she entered that very cubicle! Apparently, she was so moved by the Holy Spirit that she didn't even notice my head facing up toward her toilet.

I closed my eyes in reverent prayer just as she was lowering her panties. As she was preparing to sit upon her throne, her habit swished over my face which brought me to attention. I opened my eyes by reflex. Boy, did I get an eyeful and I do mean boy! Sister Samantha wasn't a woman! Lord, have mercy!

Well! It was a rather awkward situation to say the least! I had learned of Sister Samantha's incredible secret. I also needed her help. What could I do, but gently murmur, "Please help me, Sister. I've fallen and I can't get up."

Let me tell you, Sister Samantha might not have been a woman, but she let out a high-pitched scream that sounded like a woman giving birth. She jumped off her pot and she whooshed her habit off my pleading face. If anyone else could have seen us at that very moment, I'm sure that both of our faces would have appeared beet red.

Well! If either of us had had a blackmailing bone in our bodies, we both would have had sufficient ammunition to use against the other. Suffice it to say, each of us took a higher path except Sister Samantha had the higher advantage at that moment.

Well, that little woman proved to be very strong. She grabbed me under my arms. Then, she pulled me right under the partition of cubicle number three and out onto the restroom floor.

Even though I was feeling very shaky, in more ways than one, I managed to get myself up and onto my wobbly legs. Well, what could I say besides, "Thank you;" however, given the situation, it seemed that something else might be in order.

I felt rather like Little Red Riding Hood when she discovered that her grandmama was actually a wolf. The nice thing about my situation was that Sister Samantha wasn't about to eat me up. I decided right then and there that I wasn't going to give her up.

"Sister," I said. "How did you ever pull it off?"

That's when she told me her story. You see, Sister Samantha just happened to have been born in the wrong body. She was really every bit as much of a woman as myself with one notable exception. God sure works in mysterious ways!

Sister Samantha was the most beautiful child. She was christened "Bobby O'Reilly" and she was her mother's only son. As it had turned out, he was her only daughter too.

Mother and child lived with Bobby's grandmother on the family farm. He was conceived on Christmas Eve and he was born on the harvest moon of the following year. It was a fruitful harvest, in more ways than one! He was his mother's pride and joy as well as being the favorite grandchild of his elderly grandmother. Little Samantha or, should I say, little Bobby was a perfect angel.

On his first day of school, his mother dressed him up in knickers and she sent him off to the Baptist academy in his hometown which was located in a little parish similar to our own. When he returned from school, both his mother and grandmother were in for a big surprise.

Little Bobby had discovered the academy's Good Will clothes closet and he had decided to change his outfit. When he returned to his grandmother's farm, he was wearing a dress, high heels, and he had braided his long locks into a perfect French braid.

Grandma O'Reilly chastened her daughter by exclaiming, "Whatever possessed you to send Bobby to school like that?"

Bobby's dumbfounded mother simply stared at her son and said, "I didn't!"

That was just the beginning. By the time Bobby was in high school, he had run off to the big city and he had started living as a woman. He had the most gorgeous natural female breasts and he began to receive hormone shots that made him the envy of the big city drag queens.

He named himself Samantha Monet and he decided to seek fame and fortune as a female impersonator. With his new female voice, he could hit a high C and he was soon performing in the big city clubs and making big money.

One of his favorite routines involved him dressing as a nun. It only seemed fitting since he had converted to Catholicism and he had decided that, once he'd had a taste of the world, he was going to become a nun. Sister Samantha was a smashing success as she wooed the crowds with her renditions of religious songs that soon won converts to her beloved Savior.

Sister Samantha was planning on having a sex change, but a part of her believed she was born in a man's body to teach the world a lesson in tolerance of those who are different from others. Well! Sister Samantha had already taught me a lesson! T-LIAM-G!

By the time Sister Samantha had made a mark for herself in the big city, she quietly disappeared to the Sisters of Charity and she took her vows as a nun. When the call went out from the Have A Heart convent for new blood, Sister Samantha was ready to leave the big city behind. She was ready to follow her passion of compassion for those in need, indeed.

She had become a nurse and she was taking a mail order course in veterinary science. She was ready to serve both "man" and "beast." That's the long and short of it and we were now the lucky benefactors of her talents. Her secret would be safe with me; and, I trust that her secret will just be between you and me as well as the lamp post of eternal light.

Chapter 26

Meanwhile, life on Dinkledorf Drive was just as crazy as ever. Dinkledorf Drive had been named in honor of Poopsy Dinkledorf's grandfather, Puddles Dinkledorf; he'd been the first Dinkledorf in our parish. That was the beginning of great mayhem and we can thank the relative newcomers of the Mayhem clan for providing more than their share of that.

As for now, I had my own calling. It was time for me to confront Mark Mayhem about his transgressions against man and woman. This also meant that I had the onerous task of letting Marjorine Mayhem know that she was married to a closet case. Lord, give me strength!

I arrived at the Mayhem residence just as Mark was going out the front door. I decided to take the bull by the horns and I called out to him, "Mark Maketh Mayhem, When are you going to decide which way the wind blows past your lower nature? You've been making a fool of your wife and you've inflicted a blow on the soul of your friend, Diddles. Enough is enough! It's time for you to act like a man instead of a beast."

Mark simply hung his head in shame and he slunk away like the naughty little boy like whom he'd been behaving for the last fifty-some odd years. If he couldn't answer to me, he'd have to answer to God from whom he could never run. Well! If I couldn't make him wake up and smell the whiskey, I could at least spare Marjorine the ongoing pain of having to live a lie.

I knocked on the door and I waited. In due time, Marjorine answered the door, dressed in a simple frock. She looked as if she was ready to go to a high school dance but had instead been stood up by her suitor. My heart went out to her.

She said, "Sister, if I'd known you were coming, I would have baked a cake."

I said to her, "Dear sweet Marjorine, that's not necessary. I am here on a mission of mercy."

Marjorine looked like the confused schoolgirl she had always remained. She invited me into her immaculately kept home where I sat down in one of her comfortably overstuffed chairs. I asked if I might have some refreshment. This was no time for pretense and I needed all the strength I could get. She asked me if I would like a nice cup of tea, but I suggested that a tall tumbler of bourbon would be even more welcome. Desperate times call for desperate measures!

She returned with the tumbler and I must say that I was most grateful that she brought along the entire bottle and plopped it down right next to my glass. She must have known how thirsty I was! I took a long, deliberate swallow. Then, I began. "My dear Marjorine, you look troubled."

She replied, "I just don't know what to do. No matter what I say or do, Mark is moody and keeps his distance from me. I've tried to be the perfect wife, but that just doesn't seem to be good enough."

I continued by saying, "Marjorine, there's really nothing you can do. You see, my dear. You are married to a boar who doesn't know which side of his bread is supposed to be spread with margarine; or with Marjorine in your case.

Mark is a homosexual."

"Oh no, sister!" She replied. "You're all wrong! Mark is a manly man. It's just that he doesn't seem interested in me. He hasn't made love to me in over ten years."

"That, my dear, is exactly the problem. He prefers to be diddled by a man and there's not a thing you can do to change that. He's a closet case and he is living a lie."

"Not to be rude, Sister," she said, "but that's not what I wanted to hear!"

I persisted, "Well, my dear, then it's time for you to wake up and smell the whiskey! You can continue to bury your head in the sand, but it will bring you nothing but misery. If you want to be happy, you must consider letting him go. It's the only way, my dear."

Marjorine broke down into a virtual waterfall of tears. There wasn't much I could do except to take another slug of refreshment and give her a big hug.

I said, "Now, now, Marjorine. You're going to be all right. At least you've been blessed with children and grandchildren who can be a source of consolation to you. Remember, God never gives any of us any more than we can handle. This will just be your cross to bear. In time, you'll heal and find peace."

Suddenly, Marjorine became a bit testy. She retorted, "How can I find comfort if this is true? You say that you've come to help me, but I only feel worse. Where is the God in all of this? If you think that you've done me a favor, Sister, you're sadly mistaken. I didn't want to know any of this! Now, I'm glad I didn't bake you a cake! I'd appreciate it if you'd just leave."

Well! It appeared that I'd just received my own lesson in Remedial Holiness. Some folks just prefer to remain in the dark. It wasn't any of my business to meddle. Perhaps I'd inflicted harm where I shouldn't have been treading. Forgive me Lord.

I emptied that tumbler and I stared wistfully at the bottle. Then, I took my leave. Marjorine would have to deal with her new knowledge if she was going to come to a place of acceptance. I'd dropped a bombshell and she simply wasn't ready to deal with it.

I walked back out into the cold of winter and I wondered what I could do next. That's when I heard some loud shouts coming from the direction of Martha Mayhem's home. I looked through the tranquility of the gently falling snow and I spotted Poopsy Dinkledorf. He was peering through Martha's bathroom window.

Just then, the bathroom window was suddenly flung open and out popped Martha through the window with her wet head of stringy, gray hair. She reached out of that window with her pendulous breasts swaying to and fro with bright red goosebumps popping out all over. Then, she pushed Poopsy right over into a snow bank.

The old man let out a series of "tee-hee-hees" before he realized that he was stuck and he couldn't get up. God had opened a window and it was time for me to take some action unless I allowed that old man to freeze to death. Martha wasn't about ready to come to his aid. She slammed her bathroom window shut. Then, I approached the old man.

"Poopsy Puddles Dinkledorf! You're behaving like a naughty little boy! When will you ever learn? I'll help you get up on one condition. It's high time that you acted like a gentleman and give Martha an apology for your ungentlemanly behavior."

I grabbed the old man under his scrawny arms and I hoisted him onto his tottering feet. Then, I marched him to Martha's front door just as I heard loud voices coming from the front door of Jules Jesslike Pappas' house.

Before I could blink an eye, I heard another front door slam and I saw Marjorine Mayhem storm out of her house with a suitcase. She glanced over at me and she cast me a glare that had nothing to do with the Holy Spirit. Then, she got into her car and she gave it the gas, backing right into a snowbank. Lord, did I ever have my work cut out for me today!

Marjorine was getting nowhere fast as I heard her car wheels spinning and digging her car further into the icy snow. In the meantime, I noticed another head pop up through the parted blinds of the living room window of Priscilla Bunhead's home. She looked in my direction with her bald pate reflecting the glare of the white snow like a spotlight. As soon as she spotted me, she disappeared like a scared bunny rabbit.

Before I could decide what to do next, I heard the bellowing of Lula Mae Bunsaplenty. Not even the blanket of the fallen snow could muffle her angry tones. She shouted at the departing Jules, "Y'all can jes go an' has a slice of Mildred Mayflower's hot apple pie cuz yo' not goinna git nothing hot in dis house tidday!"

Well! There I was with that tottering old man, watching one car spin in the snow while the car driven by Jules pulled out of the house across the street. I could see that it was high time for a class in Remedial Holiness on Dinkledorf Drive. All of these adults were behaving more like children than children!

That's when I decided it was time to get back to the warm comfort of the confessional where I could tie one on with Father Cowberries. I'd leave God's children to fend for themselves. I was getting mighty thirsty!

Chapter 27

T-LIAM-G, my dears! This is Sister Mary Olga Fortitude coming to you. Now! I had a most productive confession with Father Cowberries yesterday. I certainly needed to unburden myself and we both warmed ourselves with the Holy Spirit, not to mention some other warming spirits.

Father Cowberries was able to provide me with a little light concerning the situation involving Jules, Lula Mae, and Mildred Mayflower. Apparently, Lula Mae had found out about an affair that Jules had had with Mildred some forty years ago. Why she should consider her a threat now was more than I could figure out. It seems that Lula Mae was just another insecure child of God. When will these children ever grow up?

Lula Mae had also been stirring the pot with her next-door neighbor, Martha. After I had trudged back to the convent, Lula Mae had decided to get into a little more mischief. As it had turned out, Lula Mae just happened to have seen Martha swinging her breasts in her direction, so Lula Mae had decided to accuse Martha of being a lesbian. Now, I'll back up and tell you the rest of the story as it happened.

The next thing you could have known, the two of them

were rolling around in the snow. Meanwhile, Priscilla's bunless head was taking in the sight through her parted window blinds. This only served to feed the fire. Prissy overheard Lula Mae's accusation and she decided Martha was having too good a time. Then, she started casting her own judgments concerning Martha's sexuality. She, too, decided that Martha was a lesbian.

It would just be a matter of time before the rumor mill cranked out the latest press release. Martha had been pegged. The thing is, the rumor mongers might have known something about Martha that Martha didn't even know about herself. Isn't it ironic that sometimes, we are the last to know the real truth about ourselves?

Priscilla Bunhead wasted no time. She got on the phone to Amanda Ann Adult concerning her latest suspicions about her childhood enemy, Martha. She was going to get even with that bun-lopper if it was the last thing she did.

She decided to call an emergency session of Bunheads Unite Now. Her community of lovely lasses with strangled tresses wasn't going to be safe as long as a wayward gal was on the loose. Prissy decided to "out" Martha and it wasn't going to be a pretty sight!

The hastily arranged meeting was held in Prissy's living room that very night. The Mayhem sisters and granddaughters were in attendance. Even Lucy Lovely attended. Woe is me! Perhaps I'd lost her to the dark side.

Priscilla had her own agenda. Martha Mayhem was going to pay. Prissy was going to protect her bunheads against evil influences and Martha would become her unwitting victim.

Fortunately, I caught wind of this sordid affair and I spoke with Sister Samantha. The two of us came up with a plan. Sister Samantha would infiltrate the hate-mongers and she would attend the meeting incognito.

If anyone had been taking a stroll down Dinkledorf

Drive on that dark and dreadful evening, they'd have been able to hear a drumbeat cadence. The indoctrinated women of Bucksnort were mindlessly chanting, "Bunheads Unite Now! Bunheads Unite Now!"

That's when Priscilla stood up to the podium and began her rabid recitations to her adoring masses. She cried out, "There's an evil in our community that dares not speak its name. It slinks through the cover of night and it threatens womanhood everywhere. It lops off beautiful buns and it seeks to subvert the chaste as well as the betrothed. It poses as purity, but it is a perversion. It calls itself, 'Lesbianism!'"

An audible shudder went up from the assemblage of the twisted bunheads. Lucy Lovely squirmed in her seat. She soon had company when the daughters of Mayhem, Mayflower, and Merriweather gyrated in their own seats as the call for purity went out.

Priscilla painted her picture of perversion as she built to a feverish pitch, "Let the call go out! It's time to send those lezzies back to the Isle of Lesbos! Bunheads Unite Now!"

That's when Prissy called for a volunteer to spearhead her Mission Against Martha which she planned to call "MAM." She was ready to form a new society and she needed someone to do her evil bidding. All eyes were glued upon the hand that was raised. It was none other than the hand of my own hopeful, the precious Lucy Lovely.

Just then, another hand trumpeted to the top. Grace was on hand and that hand belonged to Sister Samantha. She wasn't about to let this lynch mob trample on one of the faithful. Even the Martha Mayhems of this world needed protection and understanding. Sister Samantha had already experienced her share of the evils of judgment and misunderstanding. If you'll pardon the expression, she wasn't about to put up with this shit! Lucy Lovely quickly lowered her hand as Sister Samantha stood to face the lioness. Sister Samantha spoke quietly and deliberately as she said, "Priscilla Bunhead. You call yourself a Christian, but you are nothing more than a Pharisee. You call something you don't understand an evil, but you are the one committing the greater sin. All is fair in love and there is nothing lovely about what you are proposing. Let the shame be on you and anyone who would support your call for prejudice."

For nearly the first time in her life, Priscilla Bunhead was speechless. Her wayward and fake bun sat askew on her bald pate. Sister Samantha had made her mark as she called for compassion. Even Lucy Lovely realized her mistake. All the assembled bunheads hung their heads in red-faced shame; that is, all of them except for prissy Priscilla.

Having said her piece, Sister Samantha radiantly rose up from her seat. Then, she left the bunheads to their own devices. They would have to answer to God and no excuse would do. God knew that they had been up to no good. Martha would be let off the hook, at least for now.

Chapter 28

A letter to Lucy Lovely

T-LIAM-G, my dear! This is Sister Mary Olga Fortitude coming to you. Now! I'm writing you to express my concerns for what has come to my attention as your less than holy behavior. Mind you, my dear, it's not my intention to shame you. I just wanted to wake you up to your spirit in hopes that you will get back on the High Way to God.

I haven't seen you in my recent classes in Advanced Holiness which I must confess has caused me some grave concern. What is even more concerning is the report that I've received from Sister Samantha Monet that you have been persisting in your bunhead ways. I believe that this can lead to nothing but trouble.

After all, my dear, His-story is filled with movements that have worked up people into a frenzy of witch hunts which have resulted in persecution and mindless murders. These dark moments have done nothing to lead the righteous over the rainbow of hope. We all must remember that the road to hell is paved with good intentions; however, we must be right-minded. That means that we need to remain open-minded concerning others who are different from ourselves.

All humans are unwitting victims of our egos and the sin of judgment. Surely, you know this to be true. After all, you are a blessed and truly beloved child of God.

In practicing the Golden Rule, we must necessarily guard ourselves against the evils of the world. There are too many monkeys who forget the need for vigilance against seeing evil, hearing evil, or speaking evil. Gossip and rumors only feed the fires. I say enough is enough!

When we strangle our temples with tight little buns, we can no longer think for ourselves. It simply serves to cut off the connection to our hearts. When shall we ever learn?

I'm going to say some things to you which might disturb your past view of the world. Let's face it, my dear. Life can be messy! The only thing that we create by clinging to all of the wrong programming we may have received is a sense of fear rather than love. Let us be present to the moment. Let us only see and practice love.

Unfortunately, my dear, a lot of that comes from our own past religious programming which has led us to feel ashamed about who we really are. God knows, even I have been a victim of this. It is our task to discern right from wrong. I truly believe that that is not the case for you. If only all of us follow the Golden Rule without getting caught up with all of the complications that man is capable of devising, we'll be back on the pathway to illumination.

To put it simply, we must surrender to a power greater than ourselves which is only about love. The fear of God is a paradox that the blind cannot see. I believe that there is only fear and love. Fear comes from that devil, the ego. God is only about love. He only wants us to love and adore Him, my dear. What's more, that is the only thing which He offers to us. He loves each of us unconditionally. That is why He sent us His son, Jesus.

Jesus comes again and again in many disguises. For all you know, he may be here right now. The only thing is that he is here to teach us new lessons about love and forgiveness. Let's not kill the messenger. Let's not crucify the one whom we consider to be our Savior again.

There are too many statues to the one many of us consider to be our Messiah. That is also the case with all of the dead prophets and saints. Let us honor the living so that we may all be born again to eternal life.

Let your love flow along with those beautiful tresses with which God has blessed you. There is nothing to be ashamed about when it comes to physical beauty unless one becomes vain. Beauty is as beauty does.

The Lord wants you to be happy, joyous, and free. Consider the lilies of the field and the birds of the air. They are simple reminders from God that the best things in life are free. Let us learn from nature. In order to lead a good life, it is important to Keep It Simple Sweetheart; and, that translates to "KISS." Let us love and forgive ourselves. Let us love and forgive one another

So, my dear, seek the truth and the truth shall set you free. Then, you will find lasting happiness and a love that no money could ever buy. I'm not saying that you have to cut off your locks, put on a wimple and habit, and join a convent. I'm just asking that you join the celebration called "Life."

You know right from wrong. You can and you have served as an inspiration to others. All you need to do is to keep your eyes on the gold which is GOD. Good orderly living will always lead you in the right direction. When you are firmly on the path, you can testify to his Amazing Grace. All you need to do is to serve as an example; and that, my dear, will plant those little seeds of hope within others.

When you are ready, I am asking you to come back to our class in Advanced Holiness. Miracles happen every day and I still have faith that you will become a strong teacher. I only hope that I've given you some food for thought. In the meantime, look to the rainbow of love and you will find your way to a lasting peace. Surely, my dear, you deserve it!

Love always,
Sister Mary Olga Fortitude

Chapter 29

Meanwhile back on Dinkledorf Drive, Marjorine Mayhem had once again broken down into tears as she worked her way further into a tailspin. Her plan to return to her mother had brought her to a virtual standstill in a snowbank of hopelessness. Everyone else on Dinkledorf Drive seemed oblivious to her predicament; everyone, that is, except Martha Mayhem.

Martha heard those spinning wheels and she hoped that they belonged to Priscilla Bunhead. She thought that it would serve Prissy right to get frostbite in the very spot where Martha had severed her bun knot! Martha was up for a little mischief.

First, she put on her union suit. Then, she threw on her pea coat and her ear muffs. Finally, she sneaked out through her garage to investigate. At first, she couldn't tell if the spinning wheels on the silver sedan belonged to Prissy or to her sister-in-law. They'd both bought their Chevy Luminas from Poopsy's now-deceased son, Pee Wee Dinkledorf, during the March Madness sale of 1994.

Martha trudged through the snow, as she stealthily approached that struggling car. As she peered around a snowdrift, she noticed Marjorine slumped over the steering wheel and sobbing. Martha had never been fond of her sister-in-law, but she was even less fond of her brother, Mark. After all, he was family and Martha had no lost love for the rest of her Mayhem clan. Despite her gruff exterior, Martha secretly possessed a soft spot in her heart. Even though she'd been hoping to stir up some trouble, she took pity on her sister-in-law.

Martha knocked on the car window which gave Marjorine a start. Martha motioned that she would help and she moved to the back of the stranded Lumina. This would be a time when Martha's butch manner would come in handy.

She positioned herself behind the car, took a deep breath, and she shouted to Marjorine, "Give it the gas!"

Then, Martha heaved her hulk and she gave that car a shove that could have toppled all of the Dinkledorfs like dominoes. The wheels of the car started spinning. Then, they suddenly gained ground and the car lurched forward.

Martha strode back to the driver's window and asked, "Where're you goin', Margie?"

Marjorine sniffled tearfully as she told her, "I'm off to my Mama's."

Martha exclaimed to her, "Don't be a fool, Margie! You'll never make it in this weather! Come on over to my house and I'll build a fire to warm both of our old bones." With that said, Martha hopped in Marjorine's car and the two old women headed for Martha's driveway.

Back in her home, Martha built a roaring fire while Marjorine slumped down into Martha's sofa and began to cry once more. Martha turned to her and said, "Snap out of it, Marjorine! Nothing can be so bad. What the hell is going on?"

Marjorine said, "Mark's a pervert. Sister Mary Olga came to see me this morning and told me that he's a homo!"

Martha snorted, "That figures! I always thought that

there was something queer about him."

Martha sat down next to Marjorine and she put her hefty arm around her petite sister-in-law's shoulder. She turned toward her and she embraced her in a big bear hug. Marjorine responded with another waterfall of tears. Martha reached into her pea coat pocket and she took out a hankie to wipe her tears away. Before she knew what she was doing, she gave Marjorine a tender kiss right on the lips.

What happened next surprised both of these women. Both Martha and Marjorine were amazed at the warm rush of electric eroticism that swept through each of them. Before Marjorine knew what she was doing, she returned Martha's kiss and she drew her into a closer embrace.

The warmth of the fire was just the icing on the cake of which these two women were taking their first tentative and tantalizing tastes. It tasted like such sweet forbidden fruit. They both threw caution to the wind, as they began to sample the morsels of a sweetness that they had never known could have existed.

Suddenly, Marjorine felt a twinge of guilt and shame. She sat upright, as if a bolt of lightning had just passed through her. "Martha," she exclaimed, "This is wrong!"

Once again, Martha surprised herself by responding, "There's nothing wrong when it comes to love, Marjorine. God has just given us a gift. The only thing that would be wrong would be for us to be ungrateful and not open it."

With that said, the two women fell into each other's arms where all of the coldness in their hearts and bodies melted away with the flames of their quickening passion. They had both made new discoveries about themselves that morning. The love that dared not speak its name had opened their eyes. They were sisters in more ways than one. Blessed be the ties that bind and they were ready to weave a new tapestry! They would call it "Beauty." For

Martha, the beast was gone.

Priscilla Bunhead and Lula Mae Bunsaplenty had been right about one thing. Martha was a lesbian. Apparently, Marjorine was too. The newly-formed triangle which included Martha's brother who just happened to be Marjorine's husband, Mark, would be the start of more mayhem. As Sister Sledge, herself, might say, "The Mayhem's were indeed 'family!'"

Chapter 30

T-LIAM-G, my dears! This is Sister Mary Olga Fortitude coming to you. Now! Some big goings-on had developed at the convent while I was paying a sisterly call on the Mayhems. Mother Carmen had received a call from her own mother. She told Mother Carmen that she was dying. She asked her only daughter, our Reverend Mother, to come home and care for her.

Well, that meant that someone would have to be put in charge while Mother Carmen was away. Nobody wanted the job except for me. I must confess, I had developed quite a chip on my shoulder when I had been passed over for the promotion to Reverend Mother back in 1989. This would be a chance for me to prove my medal.

I must say, I thought more of Mother Carmen than I thought I did when she decided to give the job to me. My new position would be quite a challenge, though. Not only would I be serving as acting Reverend Mother, but I would still have my classes at the academy in addition to my classes in Advanced Holiness.

Well, three was now my favorite number; so, I would rise to the challenge. God, would I ever need my nightly sessions with Father Cowberries! Even so, I needed to remember that I was blessed in the simple ways and that

God would never give me any more than I could handle.

What happened next was that my classes in Advanced Holiness began to go more smoothly. There must be something to this Reverend Mother stuff! Of course, the dear children continued to be an ongoing challenge. Fartley Dinkledorf was always one to stir the air with his flatulent ways. Lord, have mercy!

I was pleasantly surprised to see Lucy Lovely return to class wearing her flowing tresses. I had a new confidence that the bunheads of this world wouldn't strangle her holy connection. I'm sure that she had finally truly accepted that she was a beloved child of God. I was also amazed at the change that had come over Martha and Marjorine Mayhem. Martha had seemingly become Marjorine's protector.

The two of them would come into class with beaming smiles. Something good and holy must have possessed them, but they seemed to make Lucy Lovely a wee bit uncomfortable. She kept her polite distance from them, going so far as to sit next to Poopsy Dinkledorf. I decided to give him a break and let him attend class in spite of his recent outburst. Perhaps you can teach an old dog new tricks!

Well, the Lord giveth and the Lord taketh away. Two weeks after Mother Carmen took her leave, Sister Shakesalot was called home to heaven. God rest her soul. She passed away during a state of holy rapture. At evening vespers on Saint Valentine's Day, she led the other swaying sisters in a hallowed song and dance rendition of the "Our Father." When she reached the high note of "forever," she lurched forward and she fell flat on her face before the "Amen." Our Shaker sister had shaken her way to the very end.

Since we didn't have the new-fangled equipment needed to open a grave in the frozen parish cemetery, Randy

Cowboy stashed her body in a snowbank. Wouldn't you know it, but we had a thaw that February! As the snow began to melt, her beatific face poked out of the snowbank with the snow melt on her cheeks resembling tears of ecstasy on her upturned face.

Little Dewdrop Dinkledorf made the discovery. She came running into the academy and she exclaimed, "Sister, there's an angel stuck in the snowbank!"

Well! I had to come up with a new solution for storing her body since Mother Carmen had planned to return to attend the funeral mass. I had Randy Cowboy move the body once again. I decided the best place to stash it would be in the convent's deep freezer. Little did I know that Sister Samantha made a habit of making a midnight raid in order to satisfy her addiction to ice cream.

I was having a refreshing visit with Father Cowberries in his confessional when I heard the blood-curdling scream of what I imagined to be a banshee. Sister Samantha had hit a sustained high C that echoed throughout the halls of the convent. It was a scream that could have raised the dead.

Quite frankly, I'm surprised that Sister Daniella Shakesalot didn't rise off her shelf in the freezer and reenact her final dance of ecstasy. Her resurrection and ascension would have assured her of sainthood. Alas, her body would soon be interred in our humble parish cemetery as soon as Mother Carmen returned. The ground had begun to thaw enough in order to dig her a grave.

Well! I took a chill pill and I rested assured that Sister Daniella would remain in a most solid state until she found her final resting place. What I didn't count on was that Mother Carmen would make her return on an evening two days before the scheduled funeral. Lord, have mercy!

I was taking a moonlit stroll down memory lane on the evening of her unexpected return. I'd been having nostalgic thoughts of my earlier holy aspirations about becoming the Reverend Mother. As I offered up my smoke-signaling prayers with massive quantities of my delicious Marlboros, I came upon the abandoned privy. I was moved to enter and seek solace in there.

Oh my dears! The memories of my youth flooded back like a brilliant prismatic sunburst. I knelt in the privy chapel and I reverently kissed my crucifix before entering into a state of deep meditation. I entered a state of holy transcendence and I began my spiritual journey back to God until another shrill high C brought me crashing back to reality.

Mother Carmen had been hungry after her long journey and she had ventured into the convent freezer. By the time I had hastened back to the convent, Mother was seemingly reenacting one of Sister Daniella's Shaker dances; however, the look on her face had nothing to do with rapturous bliss!

Mother Carmen would just be staying for three days. She had planned to return to her own ailing mother on the morning after Sister Daniella's funeral. I would still remain in the revered position of acting Mother until Mother's mother returned to God. Lord, have mercy!

In the meantime, we all had much to do for the upcoming funeral. Amanda Ann Adult would be catering for the wake. What I hadn't considered was the necessity of allowing an adequate thawing period in order to warm our honored sister's body for the upcoming prayer vigil and viewing in the parish chapel. The only suggestion that made sense was to "roast" Sister Daniella back to a moderate state of done-ness before she was dispatched to the winter of her earthly life.

Once again, Randy Cowboy was on hand to remove her body. This time, it would be into the convent ovens. Now! I'd never mastered the culinary arts; so, I had to take a guess at the proper temperature at which to roast our dearly departed. I thought that we'd better crank up the oven to the hilt. Sister Daniella was as stiff as an ice sculpture. Randy reverently loaded our over-sized icicle into the convent oven and I set the dial at five hundred degrees.

Little did I know that Amanda Ann was planning on baking cakes and pies for the wake that very evening. When she arrived at the kitchen, she began to fume when she encountered the aroma of roasting meat. "How dare anyone start the cooking without me!" she thought.

She marched up to that oven door and she threw it open with a vengeance that would only backfire on her. Her exertions activated the rolling rack of the oven; and, out popped Sister Daniella who was as well-done as a pot roast. That made the third time in three days that a high C was hit in the convent.

Unfortunately, Sister Daniella was in no shape for a viewing. She appeared rather like the work of one of Randy Cowboy's backyard barbecues. Her simple pine casket would remain closed for the prayer vigil.

The other unfortunate aspect of her vigil was that the smell of rotting meat ruined the appetites of all the faithful mourners. Amanda Ann was not amused. Her trays of food were barely touched.

On the other hand, we had a ready offering for the poor and hungry souls of Bucksnort. On the day that Mother Carmen departed, the Have A Heart Convent hosted a memorial meal for the less fortunate. Oh yes! The Lord works in mysterious ways. That would have pleased Sister Daniella a lot!

Chapter 31

*F*ather Cowberries was especially busy as the Lenten season began. There was an exceptionally large number of people who required his services in the confessional. I, myself, helped him out by serving the overflow. That's how I managed to get up to speed on some of the recent doings on Dinkledorf Drive.

The other thing that was especially gratifying to me was that some of my newest students in Advanced Holiness stopped by the Mother's chambers. One of them was an elderly Jewish cabinet maker. The other was an Islamic shopkeeper. They, too, had their own confessions to make.

Now! Getting back to those dillies on Dinkledorf Drive, the first confessor was none other than Mark Mayhem. I must say that his confession was somewhat lackluster. The basic gist of his "I'm sorries" was that he was an uncomfortable occupant of the pity pot that Marjorine had left behind.

Marjorine had pulled the carpet out from under Mark when she had moved across the street and moved in with his oldest sister, Martha. Mark didn't know what to make of their increasingly open relationship. All he knew was that it made him squirm.

What really caused him a great deal of deserved

discomfort, if I don't mind saying so myself, was that he was in a real tizzy concerning his own sexuality and his sense of masculinity. First, his childhood friend and "good buddy," Diddles, had informed him that he was done with diddling Mark; that what he wanted to do now was to make love to him. Well! That made Mark feel as if Diddles wanted to treat him like a woman.

The next blow came from Marjorine who had cast her judgment that he was nothing but a pervert. The final blow came when Marjorine left him for another woman; and, she just happened to be his sister!

Marjorine wasted no time before she declared that she was a lesbian. Well, if Marjorine was a lesbian, what did that make Mark? He truly didn't know which side of his bread was spread with margarine, or Marjorine, anymore. Poor Mark!

I much preferred the confessions of Martha and Marjorine. While Marjorine confessed that she'd broken her marriage vows, she had come to the realization that her marriage to Mark was nothing but a sham. What she had found in its place was true love as well as a chance for happiness.

The biggest miracle on Dinkledorf Drive was the change that had come over Martha Mayhem. Even though she still had a lifetime of laundering to do regarding resentments that she had toward her family and Priscilla Bunhead, she was suddenly possessed of a new spirit. God sure works in mysterious ways!

Lula Mae Bunsaplenty came to confess that she had been a gold-digger when she had saddled up with Jules Jesslike Pappas. She also confessed to the sin of envy regarding Mildred Mayflower. Her possessiveness toward Jules was only serving to drive him into the arms of a woman to whom he hadn't given a second thought in over forty years. Let's just say that Mark Mayhem had plenty of company on the pity pot. Hopefully, the added weight of Lula Mae's transgressions wouldn't make the pot runneth over.

There was one resident of Dinkledorf Drive who apparently didn't think she had anything to which she needed to confess. Guess who that was? It was none other than our own bunless bunhead!

As a matter of fact, I have reason to believe that she's about to launch another lynch mob despite Sister Samantha's infiltration of Bunheads Unite Now. That just goes to show where self-righteousness and prejudice can lead. It's a short and jagged, dark pathway to the dungeon of eternal darkness. If Priscilla Bunhead doesn't wake up and smell the coffee, she might just be in for a nasty little surprise in the end!

Thank the Lord for the diversity of people! Our little community is far from cosmopolitan, but we have a smattering of different races and religions among the other lily-white Christians of our community. We have a small population of Jews and Moslems; we have a few African-American residents; and, our rapidly opening closet is unveiling a rich population of gay people, not to mention our own transgendered Sister Samantha. I'll have to get to her confession later on.

Harvey Gossipsabitz had his own confession to make. Harvey confessed that he'd opened his big mouth to another big mouth who was doing a little more digging in the dirt, not to mention a little hopeful gold-digging.

Even though Lula Mae Bunsaplenty didn't care much for Jews, she had stopped by Harvey's shop to buy a birthday present for Jules' upcoming eighty-fifth birthday. She wanted to purchase an exquisite jewelry cabinet that would be just perfect to house the jewels that she hoped her honey would buy for her. That's when Harvey had told her about Jules' affair with Mildred Mayflower.

Jules had stopped by the young widow's home a few years after she'd buried her husband, Maynard, some forty years ago. The two of them had remained an item until the day that darling Dimples had called Jules the "N" word.

Jules had gotten mad at Mildred when she hadn't believed that her little darling was capable of being so hateful. As a result, he had decided that the Mayflower wasn't a ship upon which he wanted to sail anymore. Who could really blame him?

My next confessor was a real surprise. It was one of our token Moslems. Who says Mohamed won't come down from the mountain? Our own Mohamed Atada Mountaineed showed up at my chambers with a veritable mountain of sins to confess. The first sin to which he confessed was one involving his Jewish neighbor, Harvey. The two of them had an ongoing fight concerning the Jews' and Moslems' rights to the Holy Land.

When Harvey painted a Star of David on Mohamed's grocery store window, Mohamed retaliated by refusing to stock kosher goods in his neighborhood store. That meant that Harvey would have to travel to the Big City in order to buy his food. It also meant that the rest of the small community of Jews wouldn't find any manna from heaven in their neighborhood. Harvey quickly became ostracized and his business soon suffered.

Mohamed's next sin involved inciting the fracas at our Christmas Eve pageant. Mohamed had been well aware of Fartley Dinkledorf's flatulent ways, so he had decided to bribe him to commit an atrocity in the manger.

Mohamed promised Fartley that he'd supply him with a year's worth of baked beans and candy if Fartley would perform the dirty deed. Mohamed hadn't yet taken his first class in Advanced Holiness.

His final confession involved his sin against women. Mohamed had been a strict practitioner of treating his women like chattel. He had been initially attracted to my classes in Advanced Holiness because of Lucy Lovely. His own wife had never even dared to show her face in public and Mohamed had never seen a creature as beautiful as my precious one.

Lust had attracted him to my class, but the Holy Spirit finally brought him to his senses. First, he had become aware of his sin of lusting in his heart for Lucy Lovely. Then he realized that he had been treating his wife who was another one of God's children no better than a beast. Mohamed had seen the light and the error of his ways.

I could see that my classes in Advanced Holiness were helping to bring healing as well as understanding to those members within our community who were different from one another. My faith in man was restored once more! T-LIAM-G!

Chapter 32

*N*ow! There were two final confessions which I must
tell you about. They were the confessions of Sister
Samantha and Randy Cowboy. Let's just say that they
dovetailed perfectly. They also took us back to the scene of
a "crime" from many long years ago. That scene was none
other than that of the old mill stream.

As I told you, we had the most remarkable February
thaw. For one full week, the temperatures jumped from
zero to seventy. Then, they jumped all the way up to a
record-breaking eighty-eight degrees. Randy Cowboy may
have liked it hot; but, like Sister Samantha, he didn't cope
well when the mercury in the thermometer reached eighty-
five. Whenever that happened, they were both in need of a
little refreshment; however, their means of refreshment
was a bit different from my own!

Although it was located less than a mile away from the
convent, very few people knew about the refreshing waters
of the old mill stream. Randy Cowboy had discovered it
shortly after he'd come to work at the convent.

Being a nature boy and a true adventurer in every sense
of the word, he had been always looking for people with
whom he could frolic along with places that would serve
that purpose. The nearby rest area where gay men sought

out each other weren't especially fulfilling to him. He was a free spirit just like Walt Whitman; and, he preferred a natural setting where he could meet real men and just be himself.

As he had begun to explore the natural areas nearby to the convent, he had made a wonderful discovery. His hike through the meadows and woods had led him to that clearing down by the old mill stream.

It had been a beautiful sunny day when he had happened upon that clearing. The sun had been beating down upon the large rocks that were situated within the meandering stream bed. Even early birds had been singing as lazy curls of steaming heat had been radiating off the rocks.

His pulse had quickened a beat when he had next seen a tanned and muscular young man with light brown hair who had been soaking up the rays of the afternoon sun upon one of those rocks. The gorgeous god who had been sunbathing hadn't had a stitch on. That's when Randy had shouted, "Yippee-aye-eh!"

As it happened, the young man turned in the direction of Randy's exuberant shout. Then, he flashed him a smile, showing his perfectly white teeth along with dancing blue eyes that let Randy know he had found a kindred spirit. It didn't take Randy more than a fraction of a minute to shed his own clothes and join the fellow on the rock.

Well! After pleasantries were exchanged, you can just imagine what happened next; but, you didn't hear that from me! The twenty-something year-old young man's name was Bruce Friendly. Randy sure hoped he'd see him again

That was then, but this was now. Our own dear Sister Samantha also happened to be a nature girl. One moonlit eve, she didn't think that she could bear the unnatural heat within her habit any more. She took herself for a stroll, following the sound of a hoot owl, as she walked deep into the surrounding forest.

When she came upon the old mill stream, she felt as if God had granted her prayer for a break from the sweltering heat. She decided to let go of her burden and to refresh herself in the cooling waters of the stream.

Ever the demure and modest creature that she was, she wasn't about to strip down to the all-together. She looked around to assure herself that she had her privacy. Then, she raised her habit over her head and she tip-toed to the edge of the stream bed wearing nothing other than her institutional bra and her white cotton panties.

She tested those icy waters, but she decided to throw caution to the wind. She would have herself a cool down that would make her shake a lot in a manner that would have made our dearly departed Sister Daniella as pleased as punch. She uttered a prayer to our Savior. Then, she took the plunge into those ice cold waters.

Little did she know that she had company. Randy Cowboy was on his own spiritual quest following the same hooting of the owl. He just happened to arrive at the stream bed at the very moment that Sister Samantha was jumping out of the water.

The thing about white panties is that they leave nothing to the imagination once they are wet. As soon as she laid eyes upon the cowboy who was standing before her, what had been perky within her panties began to swell. This was the sight on which Randy Cowboy feasted his eyes as she emerged from the stream.

He was awestruck. Never had he seen a more beautiful creature. At first, he was confused. He hadn't recognized our dear sister and he couldn't understand why such a cherubic young god would be wearing a bra and panties. Even so, he let out a whoop and he began to shed his own clothes.

Sister Samantha shouted, "How dare you!"

Well! That didn't deter Randy for a beat. Sister Samantha's obvious state of arousal only served to spur Randy onto his latest cowboy adventure. He could also read the look in Sister Samantha's eyes. It spelled out her own state of interest in the cowboy's naked and upright form.

You see, my dears, Sister Samantha had taken some walks on the wild side back in her performing days before she had taken a vow of chastity. Always having had considered herself to be a woman, she had enjoyed the pleasure of being with a man. It's just that the only men who had been interested in her were gay men who had wanted to take a walk on the wild side themselves. Consequently, when Samantha Monet had shed her female gowns and her alter ego, Bobby O'Reilly had acted out the role of a sensuous young gay man.

In the presence of our cowboy cook, Sister Samantha now found herself in a bit of a pickle - in more ways than one, I can assure you! She remembered her all-too-human nature and she began to entertain the fantasy of being ridden into the wild west by Randy. God had made her only too human and she was about to face a test. To be or not to be was the question, but our steadfast sister took her vows very seriously. She would remain chaste and as well as remaining to be true to herself. She would have to let the cowboy go.

She ran to her habit and she threw it over her shivering body and her wet locks. Never having been one to have pled for mercy, she was going to hold her ground and make sure that Randy would keep her secret. Yet, she knew that she could hold no secrets from God and that she would have to make a quick confession. She had lusted in her heart for Randy.

Randy was also a bit perplexed. Always having been attracted to manly men, he was amazed that he had responded to Sister Samantha's all-too-real feminine aura. He'd have his own sorting out to do and he realized that I was just the one to help him.

Having spent a restless night in my convent cell that felt more like an oven, I was tossing and turning until I decided to get up and have a fervent prayer session with my pack of my trusty Marlboros and my bottle of Jack Daniels. I was walking to the abandoned privy chapel when I happened to come upon our returning sister. She would be my first visitor of the evening.

Sister Samantha saw my bottle of Jack Daniels and my pack of Marlboros and she asked if she could pray with me in a most religious manner. How could I deny the dear soul? She appeared to be sadly shaken.

Well! We didn't have to worry about stirring, not shaking. Jack was just fine as he was, right out of the bottle! I spoke to my sister, "My dear child, you seem to be troubled."

"Oh, I am, Sister Mary Olga!" she replied. "I just don't know what to do! I have had impure thoughts about Randy Cowboy and I just cannot rid my mind of his virile image. I want to remain faithful, but I am sorely tempted to part my habit for a chance at erotic ecstasy."

"Well, my child, "I responded, "There is no lurking beast within you as long as you let go with Jesus. He will soothe your troubled soul and he will provide you with an answer to every question within your heart. Get a grip and shift your focus upon the eyes of our everlasting Lord. He will deliver you from your despair."

With that said, we both offered our fragrantly fervent prayers with our trusty Marlboros and we consumed some heavenly spirits while we turned our wills over to God. I must say that the sweet surrender was absolutely delicious! Sister Samantha appeared to be much comforted. She finally left the privy chapel just moments before her tempting cowboy came strolling by.

At first, I thought I was having a holy delusion when I encountered the sadly shining eyes belonging to Randy; that was until I noticed the tears upon his face. I called out to him. Then, I asked if him if he would like to share some heavenly spirits with me and to unburden his soul. Randy thanked me and he gladly accepted my offer.

"Sister," he said. "I am confused. I always thought that I would be okay if only I could find the right man to be my partner. Now, I find myself longing for a different sort of partner; but, alas, it cannot be. She has rejected me for her God. What can I do?"

"My child," I began. "I believe that I already know what your burden is. I have seen a vision of a sad bride of Christ who has been tempted by another sort of marriage to which she cannot give herself. Be not troubled. She longs for you and she has loved you for your gentle beauty."

"Remember, my child, everything happens for a reason. It is for you to discern your way to the truth. Ask Jesus and he will lead you to the answer. Perhaps you will discover that you have already betrothed yourself to your maiden in another reality. Remember, the Kingdom of God is within you and all love is eternal. Seek and you shall find."

Randy looked at me with questioning eyes, but he realized that he would not have his answer in those wee hours of the morning. Perhaps a good night's rest would lead him toward illumination. For now, I needed to find my own rest. I decided to just camp out in the relative coolness of the privy and to find my own way to God.

Chapter 33

T-LIAM-G, my dears! This is Sister Mary Olga Fortitude coming to you. Now! I must say that thirty-three has become my most favorite number. It is the unfortunate age at which our beloved Savior was crucified. The silver lining in that dark cloud is that he shall remain forever young. He shall always be the fairest of them all. Lord, love Jesus!

With that said, I have decided to conclude my story for now. Thirty-three chapters are more than enough for you to digest in one sitting. Besides, I only hope that you will remain hungry for more. There is always plenty of food available at the Lord's table; and, God knows, there's plenty of food among the foibles of the tender sheep who reside in Bucksnort, Wisconsin!

Yes, I'm sure you are longing to find out what will become of Sister Samantha and Randy Cowboy. The cast of characters all have their unfolding stories. Will Lucy Lovely remain true to herself and forsake her bunhead ways? I'm sure that she will!

It's not that there's anything wrong with a beautiful bun in one's hair. It's just the manner in which it's inspired and how it's attached to one's hopefully-hallowed head. Let us remember that that devil, the ego, lurks around every corner when we do not practice vigilance on being true to ourselves.

Then, there's the broken heart of Diddles Dinkledorf along with Mark Mayhem's quandary concerning his broken sense of masculinity. We can thank Diddles, along with his sister and his estranged wife, for his own pickle. God only knows what our latest and formerly latent lesbians are up to.

I must say it again, God only knows what evils Prissy Bunhead will be up to next! Lord knows the influence she's had on the vulnerable female residents of Bucksnort. I wouldn't be surprised if the town got its name from the first time that a buck of either animal or human origin snorted after casting his first glance upon her scrawny bunhead. There sure had been a lot of snorting that went on that infamous night when the spotlight was thrown on Prissy's poolside pulsations!

What will become of the odd coupling of Jules Jesslike Pappas and Lula Mae Bunsaplenty? If wedding bells won't be pealing for them, there's still a wedding to be held in Mississippi, come July. Perhaps Diddles will find true love in the Big Easy after he gives away Baby Burpee to Junior Rathbone.

Speaking of babies, I shall have my ongoing responsibilities to the children and adult children at the Have A Heart convent. Children have such a habit of turning into little adults before one can blink an eye. The current generation of Dinkledorfs and Mayhems will surely only continue to test my patience as they evolve into older, but not necessarily better, versions of their young selves. There will also be other children who will come to my attention, not the least of which will be the offspring of Dimples Mayflower. That shall come another time. Lord help us all!

In the meantime, I will have to face the challenge of

being humbled since I will soon become demoted back to my simple state of grace. My role as Reverend Mother will cease and I will once again become Sister Mary Olga Fortitude when Mother Carmen Burana returns from her mother's deathbed. Yes, indeed! Life goes on..

As always, I have the Lord for my strength and I can thank Randy Cowboy and Father Cowberries for my other means of sustenance. After all, to be human is to be addicted and, Lord knows, I am no exception! I can only hope that I've offered you some morsel of hope for a better tomorrow. It will be up to you to look up to the Lord to discern whatever truth you may derive from my messages. Until then, I wish you all Godspeed along with the reminder, "T-LIAM-G!"

Love,
Sister Mary Olga Fortitude

Printed in the United States
130480LV00002B/3/P

9 781432 730475